Mara Ḥâtûn
Book I

by
Abdiya Wesab

Abdiya Wesab

TM

Copyright© 2020 Abdiya Wesab
ISBN: 978-1-7350807-2-7
Large Print Version

Mara Hâtûn

Dedication

These two books are dedicated to Sevgi.
She has a unique gift to see into the
meaning
behind what seems evident on the
surface.
As does the hero of this book.

Cover art work:
Painting of Mara Hâtûn
by Sevgi Master

See:
For copies
https://fineartamerica.com/art/sevgi+master
Back cover map:
Colored woodcut of the city
*'Constantinopel des Griechischen Keyserthumbs Hauptstatt, im
Lande Thracia am Meere Gelegen'*
by Sebastian Münster
https://cityofconstantine.com/static/images/maps/
munster_1550.jpg

Abdiya Wesab

Preface

On blustery winter days, warmth shines from Istanbul's many little *lokantas*; those mom and pop eateries which most often still are family-run. The mottled light working its way through steamy windows beckons you in. Few people look up at your arrival. The steady cadence of metal spoons to chipped china bowl is punctuated by slurps and the scraping of chairs. Otherwise, the silence is almost reverent. These wise citizens are deep into their comforting bowls of *Ezogelin* or *Mercimek Çorba* - lentil soups which have provided the mainstay of Stamboul across the centuries. Topped with mint, lemon or yogurt and a sprinkle of red pepper, they are downed with heaps of bread and followed by hot tea sucked from tiny, tulip-shaped glasses.

It has, however, become fashionable to research and serve dishes that were once most favored by Sultans. Few of the everyday restaurants can afford to dish up these elegant tastes, but certain shops are becoming known for their Knowing. Of course, there is the element of mystery and creativity which keeps a safe and respectable distance between actuality and facts. As you push the door open against the heavy wind the flavors and aura of an ancient kitchen swirl around you. Can you hear it? 'Once there was, and once there wasn't when the donkey was the town crier and the camel was the barber; it happened, it did not happen, it perhaps could have happened in the tents of our neighbors.'

So it is said that *Mutancana* served with *Keşkek* was the favorite food of Mehmet the Conqueror. Rich lamb, slow-cooked with apricots, figs, grapes, and almonds, is nestled in a bed of steaming wheat which must be mixed in a cauldron over an open fire. Two men must beat the wheat while it cooks, or it will not reach the right consistency. Butter in great quantities rounds out the dish. Seasonal sorbets and coffee tinged with pine pitch from the isle of Chios follow. The weather outside melts into oblivion. Time fades. The great fire in the corner magnetizes. The bridge between the past and present warps, and it is almost possible to feel the two are one.

As Napoleon, Emperor of France, was quoted as saying, "If the earth were a single state, Istanbul would be its capital[1]." The Ottomans had been setting sights on this city of cities for several generations already. Muhammed, the founder of Islam is even reported to have said, "Verily you shall conquer Constantinople. What a wonderful leader will her leader be, and what a wonderful army will that army be[2]!" Every Muslim man desired to be that conqueror, and Mehmed believed he was born unto that destiny.

Sultan Mehmet II marched into his freshly captured Constantinople for the coronation, bearing the sword of Muhammed in his hand[3]. He was hailed by seventy to eighty thousand Muslims who recognized him now as *Fatih*, or Conqueror. He rode straight to the church of Haghia Sophia, and after humbling himself ceremoniously in the bloody dust of battle, he ordered it converted to a mosque[4]. By June this was done and of a Friday the first Muslim prayers were held there. Fatih carried a naked sword to worship, as is proper. The victorious throng of Muslims shouted to Allah[5].

Fatih's conquest of Constantinople was a major shift in world events[6]. The Ottomans had already taken much of the Balkans. Constantinople was viewed as the last stronghold not only of

Christendom but also of the Roman-Greek world view. Education, the arts, law and order, research, science, and societal infrastructure were shifted. Rome and Vienna became the new gatekeepers of what came to be called Judeo-Christian ethics, and Europe changed significantly. While Stamboul remained the "still point of the turning world[7]", the planet had shifted on its axis.

Myths also swirl around the very name of the city. Kostantiniyye or the Arabic القسطنطينية are used in Ottoman documents, indicating that the name remained[8]. Yet other names were tossed in for consideration. Some Turkish researchers believe Mehmed himself is said to have coined the name *Islambol,* which means 'full of Islam', or *Islambul*, translated as 'find Islam', or *Islamol*, 'be a Muslim[9]'. There was also the earlier reality that to Byzantines it had been "the" city to which one went for all official business. To 'go to the City' was "*īs tīmbolī*" *or εἰς τὴν πόλιν.* Whatever it may have been called, it remained Constantinople until 1930 when Mustafa Kemal Atatürk changed it to Istanbul as part of his modern reforms[10].

Fatih set about repopulating his city. Muslims, Jews, and Christian were gathered from rural districts and resettled to grow it. Each given a specific section of town to live in, with distinct boundaries: legal, residential, and religious. Each people group was assigned a task that served the sultan's plans. Mehmed realized that Constantinople was a crucial city; finding people with previous experience and skills in commerce, transportation, and urban administration would help him succeed[11].

Those who were not Muslims were grouped into '*millets*'. This means a religious and ethnic group of people with a religion other than Islam[12]. Each *millet* was assigned a religious leader according to their tradition, elected and approved by Fatih. Mehmed himself gifted the new patriarch Gennadius his scepter and escorted him in procession to the new headquarters of the Orthodox Church. Likewise, Moshe Capsali was the Chief Rabbi, the Genoese retained a Catholic district, and the Armenians were assigned quarters as well.

Fountains and shops, markets and squares, calligraphy and music, literature and diplomacy, science and architecture, honor and culture all but crumbled in the death throes of Constantinople. Yet within several decades of the conquest, these had not only been reborn, the city pulsed in a vibrance found nowhere else on earth.

Who was this young prince of the East, and how is it that he had the wisdom to not eliminate those who were not Muslim? Who influenced his actions? Who tempered him in childhood and remained faithful in changing times? Who had a key to his heart? Who helped prepare him to be able to oversee a city at the center of the world? Who stood trustworthy at his side when leaders could trust none? Who created diplomatic bridges that shaped the next centuries?

Part I
The Key

It's gold was soft. To Olivera's eye it seemed soft enough to be malleable, yet it's sheen glowed with a strength that implied permanence. The refection was warm, remembering, as it were, whence it came, smiling perhaps at its own secret, confident of purpose. It had cleaned up well and surprised her. From the way Tamurlane had tossed it to Bayezid, she could have thought it was worthless. But Olivera had a hunch.

Abdiya Wesab

It seemed like centuries since she had heard the strange tale. Truth be told, in the swirling nature of myth and narrative, it could be just a legend. But Helena told her, and that very fact sealed it as truth in Olivera's heart, at least truth enough to remember, hold on to, treasure, ponder, and dream about.

Wouldn't you tell your friend the story which made you marvel? And Helena should know, Olivera reasoned. Her father was Magnate Konstantin Dejanović, Lord of Kyustendil[13]. And it was a story to make your heart skip a beat and wonder, it was. Helena had heard it from her stepmother Eudokia[14], whose family came from Trebizond, and who had been the widow of a Turkish Pasha. It was in her travels from Sinope and Trebizond that she happened through Constantinople, and came upon this tale.

And Helena did well in the telling of it. Her eyes shone, and the dazzling freshness of the spring afternoon around them blazoned the memory deep into Olivera's heart. It had been on just such a day as this, after the long rain, when Noah's son Japheth built a wedding chest for his oldest daughter.

Like the *ben* Noah family did, if they needed a little wood, they often used bits left from the ark. And so it was Japheth blessed his daughter with a dowry chest. He wrought the key of gold, on a chain, which she wore around her neck. Not only the chest, but also a copy of the family history, written out from the very beginning of all things. Back when God wrote down the forming of Creation, starting with, "In the beginning God...[15]", and taught Adam how to write the chapter of his own *Toladoth*, which he passed to his children, and they to theirs[16].

"Eventually this daughter moved with her husband to Thrace," Helena had said, leaning back against the cushions on her divan after offering Olivera another cup of tea, "and over time they became the Phrygian people, whose children's children started the city of Lygos[17]. Each time the oldest daughter received the chest and it's key to guard. Important historical events were added to the *Toladoth* when they took place.

One of the daughters was named Phidalia, and was queen of Lygos. When she married Byzas, they built the city with walls, and named it Byzantium. Centuries past, and the chest was lost in a war with King Darius of Persia[18]."

When Olivera heard this she nearly wept. How terrible to think of something so precious being lost! But Helena hadn't stopped her narrative. As any good minstrel would, the story must be followed, not interrupted. The key had been safe guarded, and passed from princess to daughter, saint to queen. Someone always kept it, and each generation searched for the missing chest.

Finally, when Emperor Theodosius II was excavating for the walls of Constantinople[19] the chest was discovered, and lo, the key still worked. The *Toladoth* was ancient, but amazingly, every word of the writings, from the beginning until the time of Noah was the same as the Bibles which were written out in the Scriptoriums of Byzantium. King Theodosius kept the chest safe, and his sister Pulcheria wore the necklace.

Olivera stood and went to the tent opening. She drank in the cool evening, beauty of moonrise, and awakening stars. The tinge of orange along the horizon hid behind a copse of trees. Day unto night, season unto season, the earth remained the same, while the many eras of history turned pages, but in some ways changed nothing. She was still retelling herself the story Helena had told her. Still pondering it, as she had, all her life. The Theodosian Walls of Constantinople had been built in the 5th century. How much time had rolled past since then.

As Helena told it, the key was stolen during the Fourth Crusade, the chest had been in the palace that was burned. It was rumored that a network of tunnels connected the palace with churches and it was hoped that the chest might yet be hidden, as it had been until it was found by Theodosius. But what good would that do, Helena had said, seeing as the key was gone?

Olivera opened her hand in the moonlight. The key had cleaned up well. Tamurlane's story made little sense, and there was no possible way, perhaps, of ever making the connection between a lost chest and stolen key. Who even knew this ancient myth now, besides herself? Strange though, how contented the key seemed with her. It had warmed to her touch, and if the key had had a voice, she might have thought it would say it felt safe.

The words she had pieced together from Tamurlane's telling were meager enough. A thief had been thrown at his feet, and, stammering, the man had told three tales. Clearly he knew whose presence he was in and was babbling to protect his head. His first attempt had been to offer the king an amulet that he had discovered in a chest in Jerusalem, at the back of a church. When Tamurlane didn't seemed impressed with an amulet, he claimed he was a famous gold-smith, and would make the king many keys like this one. This was just his sample. When Tamurlane glowered at him that filthy samples tell no lies, the thief had cowered lower and said the key was magical and had come from Rome. Tamurlane wanted no more of his time wasted with hot air. He had abruptly thrown the key across the room and stood to give orders for the dismissal of this captive with his head on the floor.

The key had flown across the room and hit Sultan Bayezid on the head. Fortunately he wore a turban. The key slid harmlessly down into his hand. He surreptitiously tucked it into his sleeve, and later, when back in their tent, had handed it to Olivera. His renditions of the tale were simple. He was tired. They key, the thief, and the interactions with Tamurlane were overwhelming. Olivera thanked him for the key and went about her work of ministration to his needs. His cough was getting worse, and worried her.

Part II

The Women

Stella
1418

Stella wrapped her shawl closer around her shoulders. The wind was crisp up on the terrace. It whipped around the ladder, tugging at her skirts. Tucked in her apron she had the scraps from supper. Whispering, she went from nest to nest, cooing at her birds, giving each a small portion. Their whiteness shone despite the gathering darkness. Soft beyond anything weaving cotton or baking bread could accomplish, their feathers smoothed to her touch. Eager, gentle little pecks tickled her fingers as they went for the treasures she held out to them. Cooing, they chattered to each other, content, safe, nurtured. She loved their soft eyes and the pungent, tangy smell of their cozy nest.

"Don't be long, child!" her mother's voice came from below, "it's a sharp night. Don't want you catching a chill!"

Stella knew the answer, but still, she wished she could gather her birds and bring them inside, where it was warmer. Mother kept explaining that feathers kept them warm. And, indeed, it seemed the birds were content outside in the cold. But still.

Latching the cage, she took one last glimpse of the night sky. Over the

Aegean, it was turquoise and green along the edge of blackened water. Orange streaks shot up into the approaching clouds. Yet when she turned to face east, the night had already drawn its curtains. In summer they slept out here and could breathe the air of the stars, but in winter they huddled close to the fire downstairs, where the pot bubbled and smoke cloyed. The constellations seemed further away. Maybe it was the smoke of many fires or perhaps when it was cold, stars huddled closer to heaven? Turning to head downstairs, she thought to ask Mother about it.

Ertine
1420

"Oh how pretty!" Ertine clapped her

hands and turned round and round, admiring the bright colors and the way the light caught in the jingling bells along the hem of her skirts. Her nursemaid, however, clapped her hands briskly, for her to stop.

"Ertine! That's quite enough! Really! Must you always be the center of attention? A princess must learn to be demure," she was not done.

"You forget! You received this pretty gown because you have a new baby brother. Do you hear me!" Ertine had stopped at the first sound of disapproval. She now stood, head down, before her nursemaid.

"Look at me!" The child did. "You are a girl! Never forget this! When a girl is born, the owls mourn, the spiders spin heavy webs, and the midwife is sent away unpaid." She stood up and shook her finger at Ertine. "Celebrate that you have a brother! He will be the savior of your home! He will be a hero! He will inherit your father's throne! Today we are celebrating that your mother has been given a name! She comes into the light. She has redeemed herself by bearing a son!"

Ertine still looked puzzled but kept her thoughts to herself. "Now go!" she was commanded, "take off that noisy frivolity until supper, when you shall present yourself to your parents and kiss their hands. You must keep it clean, and walk carefully. See that you do not tear anything like you usually do!"

Stella
1420

Stella hurried to keep up with Mother. It had taken longer than they had thought to gather the soap and candle making supplies in market. Thankfully the bread was baked, and the table set. Father would not be too cross, she hoped. It was Sabbath, and they knew everything must be in order at sunset, with the family gathered, and supper ready. She made herself run faster.

The vendors had been full of the bits of news one only gets in market. Perhaps that had eaten time. The "did you hears" and "don't you knows" sounded like so many chattering pigeons to Stella. She played a game with herself whenever Mother stopped to barter for beeswax or essential oils. The banter would go back and forth.

"*Ti ginete!!* How are you? It's been too long since you've shopped here. How's the Rabbi?"

"Fine, fine. Doing well."

"And your son; what do you hear from him?"

"He writes that he is doing well, thank you."

"And your Mother?"

"Thank you for your kindness in remembering her. She has had stiff knees, but still tends the goats. And your family? How are you?"

"Good, good, we are well."

"Your daughter, did she have the baby?"

"*Paidi mou*, yes, a son it is, and chubby. And such thick hair already!"

"You must be so proud. Did they name him for his grandfather?"

"Yes, and my husband can't get enough of telling of it, you know how it is."

"And your son? Did he finish his studies?"

"Yes, and so my husband is like a man who sits in the city gates, you know, with so much to boast of! *Ya ya!*"

And they would go on, and Stella would pretend they were birds, chattering. If she listened just so, their intonations sounded like pigeons when they were excited. She had to keep herself from giggling. One time she had laughed at the wrong time when the lady at the wax stall said that the neighbor's mother had died. Both women had turned to her with such surprise, she had covered her mouth and been horrified with herself, and Mother chided her all the way home.

Today they had gone on about the news. There was a rumor that the Ottomans had crossed the Dardanelles and were fighting on the Peninsula. A rumor that fighting men would have to go; that sons might be called to the front; that people were already leaving. Mother was sobered. She had stopped halfway through the normal list of purchases and done something Stella had never seen her do.

"*Éla! Éla*, Stella! Come now, quickly!"

Grabbing Stella, she went out of market, up a steep street they had never been on before and turned left along a high street. Stella was intrigued but knew better than to ask questions. The walls were high around them. Cypress trees grew in gardens nearby. Stella could tell. There was a certain way soil smelled that let her know plants were happy. The air was full of bees. Citrus and almond were in bloom and the aroma stamped itself in Stella's mind like a piece of heaven. She involuntarily slowed to breathe it in. Had that street led to heaven, maybe?

Mara Ḫâtûn

Why had they never come before?

Mother jolted her on. Moving quickly, she turned up another street that had stairs to to overcome the steep incline. Suddenly, she swerved in a doorway, and stepped into a room with high ceilings. Moving to the left, Mother picked up a candle, and walking intentionally forward, lit it from a tall candle, like Father lit the *Shamash* Servant candle at Hanukkah.

Curious, Stella watched as Mother went over and stuck her candle in some sand at the foot of a painting. Bowing her head, Mother prayed quietly, looked up at the painting, and then turned around and just as quickly, left.

Their descent back into the bustle of the market was so fast that Stella was disoriented. Almost as if it had been a dream. Mother looked at the sky, saw how late it was, and they bustled home. And only just in time. She and Mother worked quickly to get the meal on the table. Whipping the roast out of the oven, Mother placed it in the center of the table while Stella filled the hand washing bowl and got a clean towel, placing it between Mother and Father's seats on the table. The bread and wine were there, ready. The candles set. The fruit, the salad, the pickled beans, and the cake Mother had prepared were to perfection. Stella was still catching her breath from their mysterious outing. It was exciting, as if she had traveled to another world in a dream, and come back. Maybe this was what her birds did when they flew away?

They looked at each other with a sigh of relief, and then Mother surprised Stella. She looked around carefully to make sure no one was near, leaned over and whispered, "Not a word to Father about our outing today, or I'll never take you along with me again."

Halime
1422

"Princess Hatice Âlime!" the servant announced. She curtseyed with skill and moved gracefully across the wide room to be seated with aplomb next to her mother.

Abdiya Wesab

Because today's meal was strictly family the ladies were included. Otherwise, the females ate in the women's quarters. It would be crude and beneath them to expose themselves to men outside of the circle of direct relatives.

Princess Hatice Âlime was rarely called by her full and proper title. It was usually Halime, a handy blend of the two names. But she rather expected to have more formal recognition, now that she was older. She wiggled with glee in her seat, looking forward to it. She was fully seven years old now, and almost of Age.

Smoothing her crimson gown, she waited impatiently for the rest of the guests to be seated. Really! Did everyone have to be announced so? It was one thing for herself, the princess, the oldest daughter of Taceddin Ibrahim II Bey and his wife, sister to the Sultan of the Ottoman Empire, Selçuk Hâtûn. She was royalty. But the rest of these pions? She rolled her eyes and looked out the window, bored already by the airs everyone felt that had a right to.

Outside the hills of Kastamonu dappled between the blue-tinged hue of fog and the muted tone of chestnuts changing into autumn garb. Boisterous winds were switching tones, predicting tempestuous weather. Halime loved gales, especially thunderstorms. When she was younger and didn't know better, servants had to chase her back inside when the winds picked up. Something about their wild dashing drew her outside and made her want to run with them over the mountain. But now she was far too dignified for that!

With a rustle, everyone was standing. Halime quickly scrambled to her feet as well. It was her uncle, the Sultan. One must show homage to him. And she agreed. Not only was he the ruler, and therefore due the honor given, he had also been a cunning leader, and she admired that about him. Nothing stopped his advances. It seemed that there was always some new story abroad about his victories, first in Europe, then in the east.

Finally, however, the fanfare ceased and the food was served. Dusk whispered at the windows. Many candles on the table and walls danced as the servants bustled about with trays of food.

The dainty soup was warming. Halime tore off pieces of *Katmer* flatbread and dipped it in tahini and rose jelly. But she was impatient for the main meal. A platter heaped with stuffed pigeons arrived at last. Then the rice, rich with rose water, currants, and pine nuts. The whole roasted lamb was centered before the sultan, and the servants expertly carved pieces to be placed on each plate.

In between the mounds of bread, bowls of pickled mushrooms, olives, and hot sauce were circulated. Being ravenous, Halime delighted herself in the rich flavors. The pleasant contrast between the dark and cold outside and the warmth of meal and conversation within made her feel happy.

"Your *kuyu kebab* is exceptional this year, my dear," Halime's aunt murmured to Mother.

"Thank you," Selçuk Hâtûn said modestly, but Halime could tell she was pleased with the praise. It took two weeks to prepare lamb this way. As her aunt talked Halime learned that Kastamonu alone had the reputation for roasting lamb in an old well. It seemed such a sensible practice to her, knowing nothing else. She marveled that it wasn't more common. Now, if she were ever a Sultan's wife, she would see to it that the recipe went along with her!

Mara Ḫâtûn

Mara
1424

Mara smiled. It was just as the morning canticle said, the dewdrops were dancing. She hummed the tune, remembering the words by heart,

O day, arise!
Dewdrops are dancing.
Woven into the fragments of light
All of creation worships
Our creator
The uncreated, eternal, only God.
Every living being
Rises, arises, overcome with awe!
Come away, come away,
Come praise, come arise!

Abdiya Wesab

His Glory calls us higher!
His Love never fails.
His Love knits together the Way,
Calling us higher.
Woven into the fragments of light,
Dewdrops and birdsong
Dancing in praise.
O day, arise!

Skipping down the path, Mara was arrested by a feather. Chestnut and spotted, sparkling with dew and whispering her name. She picked it up cradling it in both palms as if she might damage it. Standing up, she looked for the bird who had gifted her with this treasure, but it was gone.

Her father was always pleased to see her when she came into his great study.

Sure enough, he stopped what he was doing to look at what she was holding out in her two small hands.

"A feather, Papa. Look!" she lifted it to him, "which bird is this?"

He took it over to the window to see better. "Hmmm. You see how they are spotted, dear?"

Mara nodded, "and the chestnut tinge on the one feather here," he went on.

Mara climbed up on the window seat to see better herself. "I believe you have a wing feather of the Great Spotted Cuckoo, my dear," he said, smiling, and handed it back to her. "That's a keeper!

45

These birds are the best protectors of our land."

"How, Papa?" she asked, pulling her knees up inside her skirts and hoping for a story.

He sat down on the ledge next to her. "Many other birds prefer soft food. The cuckoo, however, eats insects, spiders and hairy caterpillars which others find distasteful. They cleanse our fields and forests of creatures that are harmful and venomous."

"But I've heard that the cuckoo is a lazy bird and lays its eggs in the nests of magpies," she noted.

"Indeed she does. But this protects the magpie's young, for the chicks of the cuckoo secrete a repellent scent whenever predators come near the nest," he smiled. "You know, there is something to learn, even from these birds. The truth is, we needn't worry. God knew what He was doing when He invented birds. Every detail is worked out. And you have a feather to remind you of that now!"

He tucked the feather into her hair. "Remember the Scripture we read this morning?" he asked.

"That the same God who created us created the birds of the field and knows how to take care of them, so He will also take care of us?" she replied.

"Exactly, my dear!" he hugged her, "and that same God is always good. So remember, He gave you that feather today for a reason. He is speaking to you. He wants you to know that He is watching over you!"

She breathed deeply, leaning against his shoulder. The familiar aroma of wall germander and hyssop gently spiced the air. Mother spread these under every rug and window seat in the home, and Mara loved to help her. But Papa also had his redolence, created perhaps by the oils he applied against chilblain and cold. When she closed her eyes she could imagine herself deep in the forest, early in the morning, with dew on wintergreen, and the crisp musk of sage and thyme underfoot. She imagined a regal buck standing on the top of a windswept hill. Suddenly she had a memory.

"Papa," she began, "last night at supper, the men seemed angry. They made me feel frightened."

Despot Đurađ looked carefully at his little girl. She was only ten, but he knew that the world she lived in was fraying at the edges. She needed to know how to handle it well, and it was his task to empower her. He turned to face her, so he could give her his full attention and see how she responded.

"Do you remember hearing about your Aunt Olivera?"

She nodded, "yes, she is your mother's sister, right?"

"Yes, dear," he went on carefully, "at one point there was a war in Kosovo with the Ottomans. Your grandfather Lazar died in that battle, trying to protect Serbia. As a result, the Ottoman Sultan took his daughter Olivera to add to his *Harem*."

"What's a H*arem*, Papa?"

"A *Harem* is a place Ottomans keep their wives," he explained. "For the last 800 years, they have followed a man called Muhammed who taught that men show they're strong if they have many wives."

Mara made a face. "I don't think I should like that, Papa," she said. "I like having just you and Mother. It would be odd having many women around telling me what to do."

Father agreed, "yes, and many more brothers and sisters. I think it is rather hard on them, for the father tends to have favorites in that kind of situation, and then children can get rather mean to one another."

"But what about the men last night, Papa," she looked anxious.

"Well, the man who is Sultan now has been trying to take Greece. They have been fighting there for several years, and it is hard on the local people. When they fight, some soldiers do mean things to the farmers and their families. Sometimes they kill all the animals and burn fields and trees. This means families have nothing to eat. Some soldiers are cruel to people as well. So now many people are fleeing Greece. The men who came last night were here to tell us how things are going there."

Mara looked thoughtful. "Will we be able to take some of those people in?"

"Yes my dear, we will. That's what good leaders do. Mother will be working on that today." Father took a breath and looked carefully at Mara, "but the reason the men looked frightening to you is that the Ottomans want to come here next."

She looked up at him quickly. "Oh, that would be terrible! But I'm glad they came and told you. Now that you know, what do we do?"

"You are wise to ask," Đurađ stood up slowly and began walking up and down. The sun coming through the window cast his shadow long across the far wall. "You are third born, my dear," he said. "Your brothers are being trained to rule and to fight. Your mother is working hard to have extra supplies stored at each of the castles we rule.

"I am busy arranging conversations with other Serbian leaders and the rulers of neighboring countries. If we fight together we may be able to defend ourselves. I have also ordered the castle walls made stronger, and we are working on better water supplies."

"But what can I do, Papa," Mara asked. In her mind, she already envisioned a gathering of Lords and Knights around their hearth, like some of the ballads she had heard sung. It almost sounded exciting, but for what Papa described the soldiers doing. In the songs, troubadours told of heroes who came home with banners high and celebrations of victory. But she pulled herself back to what father was saying.

"Well, for now, it may be best if you help Mother with household tasks so she has more time for these new demands on her strength. But I also ask you, please don't go far from the house alone or with the other children. Sometimes soldiers begin wars by first sending a few men to stir up trouble, and one way to do that is to steal children."

Mara's face looked more serious than he had ever seen it. He didn't want to have to make her grow up. But times were changing, and war was pending. She would be better off told by him, and prepared, then naive and shocked. He came over and took her hands in his. "Mara, remember the feather?"

She nodded.

"I believe that God wants You to know and remember that He will always take care of us. The cuckoo may lay her eggs in magpie's nests, but the cuckoo knows who she is, and what she is meant to do. Her duties in life are different than a sparrow or a stork, but she does what she is called to do, and she does it well."

"So I will do what Mother asks me to do, and do it well, Papa. I will."

"I know you will, dear. You are the best daughter a father could wish for. But there's something else."

"Yes?" Mara looked up at him. She loved her father dearly, and her heart grew tall inside, hearing him. He was leaning against the window frame, strong, with his cape wrapped around him, ready, as he always seemed to be, for action at any moment.

"If war comes suddenly, and things happen differently than we had hoped and dreamed, never forget who loves you. I will talk with the whole family tonight on this subject. But in war, I think it is hardest for the girls."

"Why, Papa?" she asked. Mara had never seen her father look so grieved.

"Because the Sultans want the girls to join their Harems," he answered.

"Oh, I see," she said slowly, "so, if war comes here, and we don't win, I would have to go to the Sultan's Harem like Aunt Olivera?"

"I hope not, dear." Father's grief had etched itself into his forehead. She longed to smooth it out and make it go away. His fists were clenched, his shoulders back. "I hope we win. But it is better that you know now then find out suddenly later. At least for you, being a princess, you would go to the Harem. For poor girls, there is only the slave market."

"Oh! I don't like war!" Mara said firmly. "That's horrid!"

"I agree, dear. I will do everything I can to prevent it. I would like you to be able to marry a Christian prince and live in a castle of your own," he said fervently. Then he took one of her little hands in both of his big ones. "But in the end, whatever happens, there is one important key."

"Yes?" she asked, looking up at her father.

"Jesus," he answered simply. "If Jesus stays living in your heart He goes with you to palace or castle, to the north or the south. I know of men who have been thrown in jail, but Jesus went with them because He lived in them. So always keep Jesus in your heart, and He will help you through."

"So do the Ottomans follow the Lord Jesus?" Mara asked.

"No dear, they don't," Father replied, shaking his head sadly. "Their leader Muhammed started his own religion and called it Islam, which means 'to submit'. A person who follows Islam becomes what they call a Muslim. Most people don't really choose to become Muslims, they live in a land where Muslims come in and conquer, and those people who are not strong Christians or Jews become Muslims because that is what is expected of them."

"I see," Mara said, "so even if Ottomans came and took our land if we keep close to Jesus, we will find our way through."

Đurađ smiled and Mara remembered that smile breaking across the grief lines in his face for the rest of her life. It was like the sun coming out after a storm, brilliant in glory. "Yes, dear. That says it all. You understand perfectly. Well done."

That night Đurađ gathered the family and read from the Bible as he always did. Mara sat near the fire, knitting in hand, watching the flames play about the logs. The wood sighed and little caverns of deeper orange appeared hiding behind the flames. Father read from the thirteenth chapter in Matthew about the wheat and darnel. The children were intrigued.

"So are darnel poisonous weeds?" Stefan asked, looking up from the staff handle he was carving.

"I think he should just burn the field and start over!" said Lazar decisively slapping his hand into his fist.

"That's not nice. How'd he get in?" Katarina piped up.

Father raised an eyebrow and read on.

"Darnel looks exactly like wheat from the edge of the field," Grgur noted when he was done.

"And its seed is poisonous?" Stefan asked again.

"So is it about us people and the choices we make, even the little choices that grow up into big things?" Mara asked.

"Yes, Mara," Father responded. "I like how thoughtful the Master is. He didn't let the servants uproot the weeds, to protect the wheat. He let them both grow side by side until it was time for harvest. Then they were separated based on their fruit."

"Papa" Mara started, "I've been thinking all afternoon of what you told me today. Could you ... I mean if there is a war ..."

"Yes dear," Father nodded, "let me explain." He turned to the rest of the family. The details of castle walls, fortification, supplies, and weapons were outlined. He reiterated to them all that they were to stay close to the house and come inside immediately if strangers were seen, even if they looked friendly.

Mara shivered, even though she was right by the fire. A log splintered, sending sparks to the back of the fireplace. She remembered Father's words about burning fields and capturing children.

"But why don't we men all go and fight the Ottomans in Greece?" Lazar said.

Father held back a smile. Lazar was barely eight. "We might, son," he responded, "but we want to make sure that we've done all we need to do here first. An enemy typically tries to draw people out away from their castle, and then go in and take their land. So we will act wisely, but when called upon, we will fight."

"So, Father," Grgur rubbed his forehead, thinking, "are the Ottomans weeds?"

"Good question, son," Father responded. "At a glance, it could seem that way. But God is careful not to disturb the wheat and its journey to making fruit. I rather think that God looks at the heart. I know of a young man who was born the son of a Sultan who became a follower of Jesus. Your Aunt Olivera lived as a mother among the Ottomans and loved him as a son, even though she was not his mother. As a result, both she and he have born good fruit and are becoming ears of wheat, ready for harvest."

"So could we just make peace with the Ottomans and not have war, then?" Stefan asked.

"Would that we could, son," Đurađ replied, "but they are bent on conquest. Unfortunately, something their founder said makes them feel like they need to take over the whole world. They view their religion as something that everyone needs to follow in unison. It's exactly the opposite of what we believe."

Mara let her knitting needles fall idle in her lap. She watched Father, engrossed in his explanation. How wise he was! She hung on every word.

"The Bible makes it clear that each of us is answerable to God on our own for our own choices and our fruit," he went on, smoothing the page of the family Bible as he talked. "No one can blame anyone else when we don't succeed. But in Islam, the men say that women make them sin, so they keep the women covered up and inside to prevent sin. This never works, because men sin from what is in their hearts, not from being near a woman. They also set rules for societies so that everyone is kept tight inside those rules. They feel that peace will only come when everyone submits and follow all the rules. That's why it's called Islam."

"I see," said Grgur thoughtfully, "but it doesn't work to make people behave with rules. Like you've taught us before, we are each sinners, and can only overcome that sin by letting Jesus into our hearts. Then we want to change, and we have the Holy Spirit's indwelling power to do so. It sounds like they are missing out on Jesus."

"Never a Truer word was spoken, son!" Đurađ replied. While his countenance was sober, his deep joy in the knowledge that his children knew Truth filled his face. "So tonight, I will lead us in prayer, and this evening we will focus on the Ottomans. Let's pray in a circle. I will start, we go left, and mother ends the prayer."

He looked around. The family was ready. He lifted his hands to heaven. "Father God, we station angels around this home and property and ask for Your protection. Thank You for watching over us. Provide for us so that we may not only protect ourselves, but also give safe harbor to the refugees, and the many people of our land who look to us for protection. Keep our ears and eyes open and speak to us from Your Word and from Heaven. We want Your Kingdom here. Show us our next steps."

In her mind's eye, Mara saw the strong angels, taking their place along the wall. She felt the warmth of Holy Spirit's presence.

"Help me to be a good soldier, God," Lazar said, "and make us strong."

"Bless Father and Mother and all my family," Katarina yawned, "and keep the darnel away, in Jesus' Name."

"God, we ask for wisdom," Grgur prayed, "help us by living in us, Jesus, and speaking to our hearts. Help us to love well and be good stewards of our lives. Prepare us for the future, and touch the Ottomans with Your Light."

"God we want peace," Stefan added, "if You could just send the Ottomans away that would be nice. But if we need to fight them show us how. And help us make the walls strong and find enough to eat."

"Thank You, God, for our family," Mara said, "You have blessed us very much. You choose the family we are born in. So we are royalty. Help us to live that way and lead the people around us to make the right choices. Show us what to do next. Thank You also that we have a Bible and can read. Help us to learn Your Word so we can share it with others."

"Yes, God," Mother concluded, "You are Good. Thank You for coming to earth and sacrificing Yourself as the ransom to redeem our lives from the power of sin and death. Fill us with Your Holy Spirit and help us to bear Kingdom fruit. And touch the Ottomans, Lord. They need to hear about You. If You have ways to use us for that, do so, in Jesus' Name, Amen."

Abdiya Wesab

Father set the tone. The family responded in turn. Preparations kept them busy. Relatives came and stayed. Dignitaries from nearby nations were often up late, talking with Father. This was sometimes a delicate business, for not everyone saw eye to eye. Mother was a generous hostess, and Mara learned much at her elbow.

Aunt Olivera came for a long visit, with her sister Jelena. Mara watched them carefully. These women were intriguing. Olivera sometimes had a distant look in her eyes. She often fingered a key she wore on a chain, around her neck. Her husband, Sultan Bayezid had been captured in war by another Sultan, Timur.

"This man, Timur, was not to be trusted, my dear," Olivera explained to Mara's mother. They were taking tea in the back garden. Fresh white clover and fennel seeds were steeping in a pot. Mara was darning socks, a task she was proud she knew how to accomplish. In and out, up and down went her needle, clicking against the carved sock egg. The sun was warm in this corner of the garden and swallows darted voraciously about, consuming insects. Nearby, bees filled the oregano and comfrey, making a comfortable sound. The peace and tranquility of the garden seemed set in sharp contrast to Aunt Olivera's words.

"Timur conquered most of Asia," she went on, "from China right through into Asia Minor. He was known for his fierce violence and the expectations he set on his armies. He called himself the "Sword of Islam" and used his power to kill about seventeen million people[20]. So we were not excited to be taken prisoner by him, as you can imagine!"

Mara found it hard to envision, being in prison, and not knowing what would happen. But Aunt Olivera seemed so peaceful.

"Bayezid was already weak when we were captured. We were shown respect, for which I was grateful. I didn't expect to survive and had made my peace with the Lord. I thanked Him daily that Jesus' blood paid my debt. I only wished to share this Truth with others!"

Mara set her darning down and looked carefully at this grand lady. *"This is what royalty does,"* she said to herself, *"even though she was in prison, she was not focused on herself."*

"Unfortunately, Bayezid did not live the year. Timur was gracious, and allowed us to leave captivity, and deliver the Sultan's remains to his people. I was set free then, and came home." Olivera shook her head. Mara saw that deep behind her eyes there were pictures she didn't have words for. "I wish I could explain how big the world is. The distances we traveled, the various lands we were in, the very many different kinds of people there are. But it almost has to be experienced. Words fail me..."

Abdiya Wesab

A shiver went down Mara's spine. "*I should like to travel like that,*" she thought.

"Well I'm glad you're home, my dear," her sister patted her on the arm, "we missed you. Twelve years is a long time to be gone."

"Yes, and it's quite possible I might not have ever come back. It's certainly a Grace to me."

"Auntie," Mara asked, "that key you wear, what is it for, if I am not forward for asking?"

Aunt Olivera stopped and gave Mara her full attention. Her gaze was of one who had found a large gemstone in a desert, or a map while on quest. She looked like she had found that answer to a question she had always been asking. But Mara's mother felt only the awkward silence.

"Mara! That's impolite!" she remonstrated.

"I'm sorry," Mara whispered, hanging her head.

"No," Aunt Olivera said slowly, "Mara is the first person to ever have the courage to ask. For that bravery, child, I shall tell you about this key. But not yet. The time will make itself known."

"So what was the hardest thing, living with the Ottomans?" Mara's mother asked, trying to come back to the subject.

Olivera thought a minute. "I think the hardest bit has two parts," she said slowly. "first, it was hard being the only Christian, and not having freedom to talk about Jesus openly. They punish conversion, so anyone who chooses to follow Jesus had better be certain, for death is also a certain punishment if they are found out. But, there is a second part."

Here she paused and looked around at them all. "It's been hard coming back, and finding, as I talk with people, that so few Christians here really appreciate what Jesus offers us. So, on the one hand, over there, I was only really able to talk about Him with those who were hungry, and I had to do so in secret.

"And over here, people have many opinions and arguments; people talk about being Catholic or Orthodox, about purgatory and if one should read the Bible. They argue about icons and saints. But I encounter almost as little hunger here as I found there. This is perhaps almost harder than the first hard thing - because here we could have Jesus, but we are not choosing Him."

Mara was to remember that conversation for years. It rang in her heart and echoed. She unwrapped it and rethought it, awake and asleep. Its double curiosity dug deep inside her. On the one hand, that key. How was it that no one else had ever asked? What was it to? Why did it have a special time? But, secondly,

Mara's spirit realized that Aunt Olivera seemed to think everything hinged on hunger. Finally, she found her heart saying "Jesus, I am hungry; let me be more hungry for You!"

Halime
1424

"Well, you will most certainly want to be prepared, my dear." Halime's mother turned from the window to make sure she had her daughter's full attention. "You are royalty, and your father indicated that the Sultan, my brother, has plans to strengthen our family allegiances."

Halime read her mother's face deeper than her words. "You mean … this could only mean …"

"Yes, dear. I mean marriage. Not now. Not yet. But soon it will be advantageous, and it is wise for you to be prepared, yes?"

"Yes!" Halime clapped her hands and danced around, then stopped herself suddenly, knowing that being demure was the role of royalty. Her mother smiled patiently.

"Yes! I'm almost nine, like Aysha[21], the wife of Muhammed the prophet, peace be upon him! I will be an excellent wife to the Sultan!"

"Of course you will dear," her mother smiled again. "and that is why I want to prepare you. You need to know our family history and the significance of the authority and power that is ours."

Halime sat down next to her mother, listening carefully. She knew that her father's father, Izzeddin İsfendiyar Bey, had skillfully managed this region on the Black Sea Coast, and passed it to her father. Their palace had been built by the Byzantines but taken in battle by her powerful and victorious ancestors. Often she had sung the praise of the sword of Islam! Now she could dedicate her life to being at the forefront of this field. Her family was supremely powerful! For a time, even the Ottomans had been vassals to her people. Now allegiances formed through marriage were keeping their rulership perpetuated.

"Mother," she asked, "since you are sister of the Sultan, my marriage to him would strengthen the Dynasty, right?"

Two warring factions were united with her parent's marriage. Perhaps that stirring to fight and conquer was in her blood for this reason.

"Yes, dear," her mother nodded, "it will weave the Jandar Türkoman and the Ottomans into a strong brotherhood. Perhaps even do away with the strife of former years."

Halime glanced at her mother. It was true, her mother was a gentlewoman, and she handled her household with a kind but firm authority. Yet she knew that deep within herself was a passion to rule.

"Mother," she jumped up, excitedly, "because I'm royalty, and the marriage a chosen marriage, I'd be First Wife, right?"

"Yes dear," her mother smiled at the child's enthusiasm.

"Well then, my son would be the next Sultan," she proclaimed, suddenly realizing the outlet her zeal could have. She could dedicate her life to training her son, and then become Sultana and rule the Empire from the Harem.

"Doğmamış çocuğa don biçilmez." Her mother shook her head. "'Don't cut cloth out for a child that has not been born yet'. It's easy to dream, but we have some groundwork to lay. Now, remember, I was going to start to train you, at least a little?"

Halime reined herself in. She mustn't get ahead of herself. She was excited about her future. "Please teach me! I want to learn!"

And with that began many hours where Halime learned how the Genoese and Venetians came to port, and her father supervised all trade with them, across to China, on the Silk Trade Route. How all of Europe was beholden to them for any spice or silk; medicinal herbs and oil; all furs and animal skins; all ivory and teak. Mother explained that a good ruler needed to know what the neighbors had, and how to make a profit from it. How to maintain peace, but always, always be the strongest.

Mother showed Halime a handful of copper coins. "These are minted here, and people come across the Mediterranean, traverse the Bosphorus, and sail the Euxine to our port at Sinop to use them. Read the inscription."

Halime turned a copper coin over in her hand. There were two fish on one side, and it read *Dârü's-saâde-i Sinop* on the other.

"The Palace of Sinop," she read.

"That's right," Mother approved, "infidels come this distance and pay us our copper, in our mint, which originates from our port, at the direction of your father, because they want what we have. So you must always have something others want and are willing to pay for. The second is to charge as high as you can. Not unreasonably so, or customers leave. But high enough to make profit."

Halime nodded. Another thought crossed her mind. "And my brothers? What will become of them?"

If her son become sultan, Halime did not want him to compete with her brothers. But she didn't say this out loud.

She knew the history of her people, and how the current Sultan had had to go to war with his brothers to take the throne.

"Your brothers will remain here, at your father's side, dear," her mother explained. "Kemaleddin Ismail will rule well, being the oldest. And Kızıl Ahmed will be on standby. Because of the nature of war and defense, it's wise to have a second son in case the first, Allah forbid, should die.

"But my brother the Sultan is keen on our family being strengthened and well-knit together. We have had extensive conversations with him. Several of my half-sisters will be given to your brothers in marriage when the Sultan marries you. It will be a wonderfully grand affair!"

"Really?" Halime was starry-eyed. "Mother! This is amazing! Our family will be the strongest, most powerful family in the world!"

"Yes, dearest," her mother gave her a hug, "now, let's dream a bit. What colors would you like your wedding wardrobe to be?"

Ertine
1424

Ertine smoothed her trembling hands down over her black gown. It matched the mantle, kirtle, and headrail. She shivered. Decidedly, she didn't like black. Especially today. But she bit her tongue. In her head, she heard the voice of her nursemaid. *'It is not about you.'*

Especially today. She sighed.

Gathering herself, she went in the room. Perhaps it was the silent, heavy bustle of many women or the fact that the window was open, letting in cold air, but the aura of the room was heavy. The smell was dark and made Ertine shudder. For the first time, she was glad she was short. She couldn't see around the women, gathered around her mother's body like a group of black crows. Trembling she held back. She wanted to throw herself on her mother, her only dear mother, and will life back into her body. But knowing she couldn't, she didn't want to go anywhere near this strangeness called death.

A rough hand grabbed and pushed her to the front. Trembling, she was at the bedside. Here mother had nursed her brother; where she had become someone by bearing a son; and where she had died, bearing another daughter.

The dead baby lay next to mother too. Suddenly Ertine felt the weight of being the only living female in this family.

Stella
1424

Mother did go again, and Stella kept her secret. She was intrigued by this gateway to a whole new part of town that Mother knew to go to, and this place where Mother lit candles. It smelled like the synagogue, quiet, peaceful, and old. Stella felt angels there and loved the mystery of going. But she never asked questions.

And the war did come. And everything changed. Not at once. But Mother gathered more in the cellar and made meals simpler. Father looked grim and was often bowed down, head in his hands, in his study. Stella tiptoed past his door. Questions arose in her, but she knew to not ask. Once she had when she was younger. She wouldn't again.

Mother was glad that her sons were far away, in France, and wouldn't be drawn into this war. But Father was not well, and couldn't fight either. She heard them one night when they thought she was asleep.

"But Stella …" Mother said. That's what caught her attention.

"I know dear, I have written to Timon. If we can arrange to have her sent?"

"That would be dangerous, wouldn't it?"

Father sighed. He was so quiet Stella thought she had missed his response. They were talking about her. What were they planning? She wished they'd to ask her. She was old enough now, really… Her straw mattress crinkled as she moved, drawing herself closer to the wall, hoping to hear.

"Danger is a relative term, dear," Father finally said, "To travel across

Europe and go to France on her own is impossible. We have to wait until there is someone she can safely travel with. And now, with the many soldiers coming this way to fight, and the confusion at sea with piracy, my last hope is that Timon might …"

"Could we stay here, dear?" Mother asked hopefully. Stella knew that Mother loved this home, this city, this land. They had carefully planted and watered each tree, as one might tend to gold. Together they had measured how much taller the lemon tree was each year, how many more mulberries they could dry, and the length of the shadow cast by the Cypress. She and Mother pretended it was their own sundial.

"To stay is not wise, dear," Father sighed, "the Ottomans take slaves. Perhaps one might say fortunate is the one who survives to be their slave."

"And she is of marriageable age ..." Mother started.

"Would that we had arranged something when she was younger. Perhaps safely betrothed she could travel more freely."

"Have you no relatives near Timon, then? Should we write, is there anyone whom we might consider?"

Once again Father sighed. Stella could imagine him pulling on his long beard in his absentminded way, as he always did when he was concerned. "Dearest, you forget. Being a Rabbi in Salonica is one thing. Here our roots are ancient, and the vast gulf between us and Europe stands us in good stead. But on that mainland, a Jew is not allowed to marry, have land, or even enter cities. Sending our Stella to such treatment is unthinkable."

It was Mother's turn to be silent. Stella bit her tongue. Were there no young men at synagogue, she wanted to ask?

It was as if Father read her mind through the wall. "And you know," he went on, "we've often discussed that none of the young men here would do for her because they are all forced into this war, and a fighting man is a dead man. Not that they shall all fall," he hastened to say. Stella could imagine the look on her Mother's face. "No, God forbid! But those who are not killed in the war will be taken captive unless they escape. And any man who is cowardly enough to flee and not fight is not worthy of my daughter."

Stella leaned against the wall. Her parents had often talked about her? They discussed who she should marry? Well, maybe that's what parents did. She hadn't considered it before. And now the war was upon them. What was she to do?

Father wasn't done, "so she can't marry a local boy. She can't travel alone to get to Timon. And Timon can't come here, or he would also fight. I would take her there myself, the three of us could go, perhaps? But first I must recover from this … this …"

Mother patted him on the arm. Stella could tell from her tone of voice. She always patted Father when she was trying to comfort him. "It's going to be fine, dear. You'll be better soon, and maybe the war will end before we know it, and it will be time for weddings and celebrations. Just think, we will write Timon, he will find the perfect match for our Stella, and we will yet live to see our grandchildren."

Father was not finished. "What about your family, dear?" he said.

Mother was stunned into silence. Stella wondered why. Then, suddenly, she wondered why they had never talked about this. She didn't even know Mother had a family.

Ertine
1425

Seeing as she was the only daughter and had outgrown a nursemaid, Ertine managed fine on her own, thank you very much. Besides, she had figured out how to stay just out of sight, and thus out of mind, most of the time. This came in handy when she wanted to find out what was going on. And some days she did.

Most of the time she didn't care. She tried to not remember the times with mother, and that she was gone forever.

How could one be happy, when *kismet* had written the fate of being a motherless child, alone, and the sole female offspring of her royal father? This was nothing short of a curse upon him, and keeping her existence silent was the best way to protect herself from his anger.

Since happiness and contentment were not meant to be hers, she acquiesced to the silence and the dark clothing of mourning. Heavy and cumbersome weights had landed upon her, flying in that open window the day Mother died. Like some dark raven of misfortune, it settled with talons on her shoulder and whispered her *kismet* into her ears. Darkness suited what therefore became her purposes. She found it was helpful to be in the shadows when she went out. Often she escaped to the apple orchards. Yes, she had to find her way carefully, and leave and return at exactly the right time, but if she did, she had exquisite freedom. Here the sky was large, the wind fierce, the colors bold. Cold was sharp and heat pulsed, blossoms danced in colors that caught at her heart in strange pulling ways, almost like whispers of a life she could never have.

Ertine knew she came from a tribe of strong women. The Amazon women were in her lineage. Great families who had been dynasties under the Byzantines and Greeks were in her blood. But that was in the past. For two hundred years now the Celebrated Leadership, or

Kutlushah, of her father's tribal Turkmen tribe had been dominant.

So Ertine ran out to the trees and threw herself in the long grass at the apple's feet, watching the sky between star-shaped blossoms. The honey bees and flocks of birds kept her company, and slowly the raven grew less dominant and she grew to trust the birds she could see. With her ear to the ground, she knew the approach of any creature with feet from a distance. She knew also how to hide and flee. Keeping in the shadows, finding food for herself, maintaining independence, yet keeping herself well informed of happenings in the men's quarters was her life. It was at least the framework of her life.

Mara Hâtûn

Ertine's real-world was her imagination. Somedays she was a Genoese ship on conquest across the Black Sea. On others she was the Amazon Queen, giving orders to those beneath her rank. On windy days she was a bird, enjoying the air currents.

But today it was raining. So Ertine used it to find out what was happening. This meant creeping into nooks and crannies that afforded her the ability to hear conversations in the '*Selamlik*', as they called the men's quarters. Here it was she had learned her father's allegiance to his religion. It was a certain Muhammed he followed, Peace be Upon Him, who had brought unity to the tribes across Asia to defeat the infidel Christians. Strength was in unity and tribal order, at which he excelled. Being the Celebrated Leader, all obeyed his every order. He also knew the boundaries of his territory and showed allegiance to those who had more power. Power, she understood, was everything.

Today the talk was of apples and hazelnuts. The harvest had been tallied and her father was giving orders of which shipments were to be sold, which to be shipped abroad, which to be saved and processed, and which to be given to maintain peace with the Ottomans.

Ertine wished she could see. It would be far more interesting that way. But she could imagine. During harvest, she had to go to her beloved orchard only when the workmen were not on duty. The rich loam was kissed with over-ripe fruit buzzed about with incessant bees, striving to ferret delight from the windfall. Branches in autumn seemed to dance differently, as if they knew their work for the year was over, and they could majestically play with the gusts of winds that set their skirts swirling. In the other room the shuffling and stacking, the bowing, coming and going helped her envision the process her father was overseeing. She knew many servants were already employed shelling and cracking the nuts to prepare food for winter. A rhythmic pounding of mortar and pestle would soon start, with the delicious paste that nuts created.

But wait, had it started already? So quickly, only with her merely anticipating it? A thumping could be heard. But the rhythm was off. It sounded more like galloping. It was galloping! Someone was drawing close; a great many somebodies. Ertine checked her position. She was completely hidden, not only in a crevice but also with her head to toe chador. If an entourage with torches should pass she would be safe. She pressed her ear closer to listen.

"Master Kutlushah, your audience is requested by the Sultan's emissary, may the Sultan live forever!"

A brief silence, as every movement freeze at this announcement. The Sultan? Her father must be even more important than Ertine imagined!

"By all means, and with haste!" her father replied. Due to shuffles near to her hiding place, she knew he made hand motions to the servants. They exited with a near run toward the kitchen. Food would need to be prepared quickly.

More shuffles, a blast of some instrument, and the Emissary himself was announced. Her father responded with a welcome. How these people went on, Ertine thought. They always had to say the right things, and bow and perform a certain way, with every rule followed, or there were severe consequences, as she well knew. Bowing and scraping, greetings and questions, formalities and honor were all due and done in succession.

Abdiya Wesab

A great running of servants with trays and preparation to enter the royal chambers with perfect order was being orchestrated just around the corner. Inside the room, the polite niceties continued. But what would an emissary come for?

The rustling subsided and was replaced with the clinking of food being served. The smells going by on trays were tantalizing. Should she drift away and find food or stay and listen? As much as she like hazelnuts and apples, the talk about them had been boring. Perhaps the emissary would be too. She was about to leave when, quite clearly, she heard the man ask, point-blank,

"I understand that you have a daughter?"

Kutlushah answered slowly, calculating, "I do."

"Is she of age?" the emissary went on.

"She is the same age as Ayesha when she married Muhammed, Peace Be Upon Him," her father responded carefully.

Ertine felt she was looking in a verbal mirror. What did "of age" mean? She was nine. What did that have to do with anything?

The man went on, "The Sultan, may he live forever, is pleased with your loyalty, Kutlushah. He desires to show you special favor and extend an invitation to your daughter, that she might enter his Harem."

There was a moment's silence. The man continued, "there will be a rich reward for a man of your esteemed caliber who aligns himself in marriage with the Sultan in this fashion."

Mara
1429

Oh, in the woods
    Oh, oh, in the woods
Even on the gooseberry,"

Mara sang the old song, out in the garden, picking rosemary and hyssop for Mother,

Mara Ḥâtûn

"And the cuckoo, yes and a cuckoo
To the nest has whirled, nesting down
Yes the nest is settled.
It took off departing, yes, departing,
yes, it did. Oh, who is in my nest,
Whoever is in my nest
And his father will be?
And he called the nightingale
"I'm in your nest,
Yes, I'm your nest,
And I will be a father
To your children, and to your children
And I will be a father, in the woods
Oh, oh, in the woods …[22]"

Her basket was full, but the harvest so lightweight she swung it as she went from bush to bush. She loved this walled-in garden, safe from the war, the noise, the fears that rumored about. Ever since father had said they could not go out, she hadn't been. She didn't dare go into the fields, the forest, the river valley. Sometimes the confinement felt so imprisoning she went to the stables and hugged her favorite horse.

"Run for me, in the wild forest," she whispered in her ears, "run and breathe, pick fresh mushrooms! Gather birch bark! Make me a basket! Pick wildflowers! Climb the tree and gather fresh honey!"

And the horse looked at Mara, deep and comforting as if she understood. She nuzzled her and whinnied softly.

But at least they had this garden. Without this space, she scarce knew if she could breathe. How could one breathe except under God's great sky?

Only last night fresh refugees had arrived, wounded, with crusted blood to clean off, and foot wounds from the blisters of too far a journey. Anger and grief mingled in their eyes, woven with shadows of fear.

As the decade rounded the corner the stalemates on the lower peninsula crumbled. Salonika had fallen to the Ottomans in March, they said. Mother caught her breath, but the news came tumbling out. Her brother's family had been caught in the war. It was not yet known if any survived. Mara felt as if their family was being rolled under a giant wave.

She and mother made bandages. They cut herbs and made tinctures. Father sent a servant to gather willow. Salve was made for bones, and elixir of willow for pain.

And the Ottomans pressed on. The Peloponnesian Peninsula was ravaged at the hand of Turahan Bey, one of the Sultan's commanders. This unleashed a wave of attacks. Father was allied with the Kingdom of Hungary. The assault continued. With counsel, Father sent envoys to broker peace negotiations with Sultan Murad II. This was delicate because every other European ruler wanted to unite in war against him, yet Father could see that because of so many years of repeated defeat, there was no strength left to resist. The Prince of

Wallachia was in the Sultan's prison, Greece lay in ruins, Venice had been beaten back from the Adriatic coast, Albania was struggling with its footing.

Yes, Albania's Skanderbeg had potential but was struggling to unite minor tribes. Ottoman raids were wearing. Father said it reminded him of stories of his childhood when people hid indoors because every time they went out a fire breathing dragon would supposedly turn forests into infernos, or snatch up innocent children, and fresh terror was unleashed.

The raids became a force to be reckoned with. No one could work their fields, livestock that was not locked up was stolen. Fires were started. Children disappeared. Villages were ransacked and all women and girls captured.

Mara felt a fire rising in her innermost being. It was hard to contain, harder to describe. Many thoughts and memories, conversations and moments came together and compelled her into her father's study.

"Father," she said confidently, once she had permission to speak, "I feel that I need to step forward and be the peacemaker. I am the princess. If I step in the gap and offer to be engaged to the Sultan, would it bring peace?"

Đurađ froze as if caught in time. His mouth went dry; his scalp tingled. Memories of Olivera; the reality and finality of marriage to a Sultan; the plight of the people, and this fresh, raw courage of his daughter caught him off guard.

"Mara," he started, "Mara, I can't. You ..."

"Father, it's right. This is something only I can do, and it must be done," she said calmly. "Whole villages are suffering. Women and girls are being crushed by soldiers. Children are disappearing. I am but one small person, but if by stepping forward I stop this, then its the thing I can do. I sense that this is what royalty does for its people."

He took a deep breath. "I will ask your Mother," he said slowly, "and let's pray together. This is too much for me to take in."

So they did. The three of them sat and prayed. It was early spring. Mara looked out the window. The walls of the castle had been fortified; another tower had been added, under Mother's skilled oversight. Yet their protection meant little if the people they were there to serve were suffering. Yes, the castle could host and hide many, but even just one summer of scorched fields and threats of kidnapping and rape would stop all hope of harvest, and the ability to maintain life. It would seem best to negotiate a peaceful solution.

"Lord," Papa prayed, "we ask for Your Kingdom to come and Your will to be done, on earth, as in heaven. I confess I've wanted a Suddenly. I've wanted miracles. I've wanted You to step in and solve this. I know You're capable. You cause everything to work together for the good of those who love You and are called according to Your purposes for them. Speak to our hearts and comfort us; let us sense Your direction in this please."

"Yes, Father God," Mother went on, "we would like to choose differently for Mara, but You seem to have placed this willingness to lay her life down on her heart. We don't want to stand between her and Your will, but this is a burden we would never want to ask her to carry..."

Abdiya Wesab

Carriage wheels sounded on the stone road just out of sight around the corner of the building. Mara dismissed them, lost in an inner listening. The window faced the fruit orchard, swollen with new buds. She would miss this. Suddenly a cuckoo dropped down and settled on the branch nearest the window. She held her breath. Her father's words came back from that distant childhood which was so changed when the news of war became their daily reality. She heard the words again, resounding in her spirit, "He gave you that feather today for a reason. He is speaking to you. He wants you to know that He is watching over you!"

At that moment steps were heard in the hall. They weren't expecting anyone, but they turned to respond. The butler was at the door, holding it open, and bowing.

"I hope I am not disturbing you, my dears," Aunt Olivera bustled into the room, "I know that I usually send word that I'm coming, and then come, like normal people, but I felt an urgency from the Lord to come right away…"

Mother jumped up and ran to hug her. Mara was helping her with her wraps. Father gave directions to the butler for a substantial tea, and to build up the fire. It was quite a distance from Beška Monastery, and although spring was come, it was still cold out, and icy on the mountain roads.

"And how is Jelena? Busy I assume with writing and conducting the affairs of the monastery?" Father smiled. Aunt Jelena lived at and managed the Beška. Jelena's husband had been Đurađ of neighboring Zeta, which she now oversaw. Jelena's epistles were read in the churches as far away as Jerusalem.

"She is fine." Olivera said, sitting down, "and you, and the family?" Niceties were exchanged. The servants came in with *boza*, warmed and sprinkled with cinnamon. She sipped it and raised her eyebrows. "I see your millet harvest was good! I highly approve, well done!" She raised a mock toast and winked. *Boza* was known to warm one to the toes, but even though it was fermented, it wasn't alcoholic, making it suitable for daytime consumption.

Fresh *byrek* and pickled vegetables, sliced goat cheese and a rye loaf, plum preserves and candied green walnuts, a sherbet of last summer's sumac and a steaming plate of stuffed cabbage rolls graced the tray. Aunt Olivera went for the *byrek*. "You make the best, dear," she smiled at mother, "I think it's your secret cheese recipe, or how thin you roll your dough. I should learn how to stuff these myself one day."

Mara sat on the divan, feet pulled up under her, as she liked them. It would be rude to interrupt, but she was curious why this aunt, of all of them, would suddenly appear while praying about this step to broker peace.

"Mara," her aunt looked up sharply, "you are the reason I came."

They all stopped to look at her. She had set her plate down and was, as it were, interrupting herself in the required pleasantries of first arrival at anyone's home. "Some days ago I was burdened with a Scripture and I felt it was for you. So I prayed for you and prayed about it. I was going to write and send you a letter, but then I sensed the Lord saying that He wanted me to come and tell you myself."

The family all looked at each other. Mara held her breath. Aunt Olivera leaned forward. "As you know, I was sent as a bride to the Sultan after Father was killed in the Battle of Kosovo in 1389. Sultan Bayezid was nicknamed "Lightening" for how he was first on one battlefield, and then on the next. War was his main *raison d'être*. The years I was with him were not pleasant for me personally, but I was able to broker peace with my peace. Jesus lived in me, and I took Him wherever I went.

"The Sultan allowed my brother Lazar autonomy on our father's throne. Simply by being present and praying quietly at various events and through many situations, I know things shifted in ways that could have gone much worse. Even the last year, as captives of Timur, I sensed the Peace I carried. As a result, Timur respected Bayezid and even mourned his passing. Prior to that, they had been enemies. Through it all I was protected; and had many opportunities to sow seeds of God's love in the palace, especially with the wives and children."

She stopped, leaned back, and closed her eyes. "Then the word of the LORD came unto me, saying, before I formed thee in the belly I knew thee; and before thou came from the womb I sanctified thee, I ordained thee a prophet unto the nations. Then said I, Ah, Lord GOD! behold, I cannot speak: for I'm a child. But the LORD said unto me, Say not, I'm a child: for thou shalt go to all that I shall send thee, and whatsoever I command thee thou shalt speak. Be not afraid of their faces: for I Am with thee to deliver thee, saith the LORD. Then the LORD put forth his hand and touched my mouth. The LORD said unto me, Behold, I put my words in thy mouth. See, I have this day set thee over the nations and over the kingdoms, to root out, to pull down, to destroy, to throw down, to build, and to plant[23]."

Her voice stopped, but her words seemed to echo in the space, filling the room and growing. Mara was stunned. Her parents were speechless. A Quiet filled in behind the echo, and Mara felt the Peace of God touch her with a simple confidence and Joy. Aunt Olivera opened her eyes and looked at her. "I don't know for sure why I had to come here to say that, and why it was so urgent that I felt chased to come now, on the edge of winter, but there you have it."

Father drew in a breath. "Olivera," he explained. "when you came in, we were praying. We had no sooner asked the Lord to speak when the butler ushered you in. I am left without words."

"And," asked Olivera, "what were you praying about?" She looked at Mara.

Mara stood. Her fifteen-year-old uncertainness was gone. She was suddenly a confident woman. "I have been feeling that as princess I am to offer myself to the Sultan as a bride," she began. "I want the rape and pillaging of our nation to stop. I want peace to come, and as royalty, I believe this is my responsibility. Understandably, my parents are distressed. For some reason, I am not. I feel that there is a Call and a Purpose from God in this. Your coming, and the Living, Breathing Word of God, spoken to me in this hour is the confirmation we needed. Thank you."

Olivera's eyes grew wide. She sobered with each growing word the girl spoke. Then she stood, strode over to her niece and enveloped her in a strong embrace. For a moment Mara was a child again, breathing in the sweet smell of her aunt's rosewater perfume. Then her aunt stepped back and held her at arm's length. Her eyes were sober but bright. "You will do well, my dear. You are strong; not because you are personally or physically strong, but because of Christ in you, the Hope of Glory for all those around you."

Then Aunt Olivera reached up and unclasped the chain from around her neck. She quietly took it off and reached over, gently fastening it on Mara's neck.

"When you asked about this necklace, Mara, I knew it was ordained to be yours," she said, with a catch in her throat, "it has a way of calling forth destiny. It was a gift to me once, in a difficult hour. Now it is yours. You will wear it with honor. Sit down, dear, and I will tell you it's story."

And so Father issued the formal offer to the Sultan. The negotiations took some time, but Mara was engaged to

Sultan Murad in June. The betrothal stayed the invasion of Serbia. Raids were to stop, at the decree of the Sultan. Grgur and Stefan were recognized by the Sultan as descendants and heirs of the throne and given autonomy to rule with Father. A certain and calculated peace settled over her homeland; bargained for by her pact.

Mara's dowry included the districts of Dubočica and Toplica. The contract also included the promise that should Mara outlive the Sultan, she would be granted permission to return to her father's home.

Now that her engagement brokered peace, it was safe to go outside. Mara took deep breaths of fresh air, drinking in beauty of rolling hills and fresh green coming on trees. Her heart drank it in bittersweet farewell, knowing she might never experience summer at home, in her motherland again. She often fingered the key around her neck, wondering what it Olivera's story meant. It was enthralling, yet, in some ways overwhelming to be a princess wearing a key that had been worn for millennia. This very soil had been Phrygian. Perhaps they key had been here before?

Being able to roam freely near the rushing streams, full as they plunged from the mountains in the east, made her heart throb with the vastness of the beauty she sensed around her. Bill-clattering storks were nesting in the poplars, this was punctuated by the pee-

wit, wit wit, eeze wit hum of lapwing, mewing overhead. A spotted cuckoo swooped low, with a hairy caterpillar in its beak. Mara stopped and held her breath, remembering her feather. The magnificent, tufted creature was gone in a second, replaced by kingfishers, with bright mandibles. A Lullula lark began her song in the woods, and Mara moved on, caught up in the beauty of God's creation.

It was on one of the many strolls Mara took around the property that she asked the Lord for a favor. "If I am ever able to come home, may I have a life of celibacy, and simply enjoy the beauty of worshipping you in peace, please?" she whispered. Yet she also had a growing Peace that going into this marriage was an act of obedient worship, in a different sort of way. Yes, she might not be celibate, but she was anointed for service, and the strength for that rose in her, above and beyond the sacrifice she was making.

Stella
1430

"It's good we have an extra supply of water in our cistern, Mother." Stella noted. She was stirring freshly ground grains into yogurt water. Soaked thus, even if they couldn't cook it, it would be palatable.

"Yes," Mother's voice came muffled from the cellar, "and I've counted. We do still have five vats of cabbage pickled." Her voice sounded clearer as she came upstairs, "and the grain will hold out another month. It's good we re-chinked and limed the house so well last year. There are no signs of rats."

"The windows are boarded," she went on in her inventory, "we have fire wood, but don't dare make smoke except at night, and only if we are sure no one is around."

Stella went to the window and peered through the crack. At this moment there was nothing to see. Last night had been otherwise. Would that they had been able to get out in time! Last night the Ottoman soldiers had broken the defenses, and the commotion in the street had indicated that they were using this part of town as a path to get deeper into the Upper Section of Salonica. For now.

It was useless talking about it. There was really no where they could go. The soldiers would either pass by, and she and Mother might sit out the fight, or they would break down the barred doors and get in. Either way, their world was changed forever. Yes, they might eat for a time yet, thank God. But in the long run their future was … she didn't want to think about it.

"If Father were only still living," she heard her Mother say again. Yes, if he recovered, he would have gotten them out, to safety, somewhere. Anywhere.

And if Timon had received their letters and sent for them, they might have found passage. But they were trapped. That is how it was, and there was nothing they could do about it. Stella felt that familiar tightness in her chest.

"Mother," Stella said, "I'll run feed the birds." Wending her way up to the terrace, she didn't actually go outside. That would have been foolhardy. At the doorway was her dove cote. She knew each by name. "I'm a bird in a cage, like you, my dears," gently she stroked each white bird, and fed them, "you fly," she whispered to them, leaving the cage door ajar. "You fly to safety. I don't know where that is but you have wings. You can go."

Standing in the shadow and looking out the slits the doves used, she drew her shawl closer against the cold and rested in the comfort of their cooing. Breathing in the familiar peace she felt in their presence, she rested her heart. Scanning the little bit of city she could see from here, she noticed smoke rising in the eastern block of town. It was far enough away that she didn't fear it spreading, but if the soldiers were using fire…

Mara
1435

The marriage took place in Edirne, on the fourth of September, 1435. It was royal affair, with much intentional cordiality. The fact that a contract was being executed, that boundaries were drawn, war ended, power pawned and a royal scepter required as a pass for all future exchanges made the event a staged and sometimes awkward occasion.

Mara found the contrast staggering. Her people were starving. Here the five course meal sported bird tongue soup, paté of liver with pomegranate, quince stuffed with lamb, whole roast venison, goose and almond pilafs, sherbets and jams, relishes and dressings. Steaming trays of pelamide, mullet, turbot and bream were arranged on sliver platters as if they were swimming. Baskets of fruits, nuts and caviar were passed. The constant sprinkling of air, hands and hair with aromatic oils left Mara dizzy and overwhelmed.

Swirls of dancing girls, musicians in silks with instruments she had never heard before, and the curious addition of many caged birds who sang along to add to the celebratory air did nothing to steady her. After getting one glaring look from the Sultan's mother for starting in alarm when a basket of rose petals was thrown over her head, Mara focused on sitting demurely to gain her equilibrium.

It worked. To the onlookers Mara was regal, and kept composure. She bowed appropriately when she was decorated with the *kaşbastı*. The diadem encircled her head, embellished with a stone centered on her forehead. She later learned that this ornament indicated her rank in the Ottoman palace. It was placed upon her head like a seal, a type of final stamp to ratify the deal. The stone felt cold and foreign, but she knew that, with time it would warm because she herself would transmit warmth to it. She smiled to herself. How very like her situation this *kaşbastı* was! She was outside coming in. She would warm to her situation and make her new situation a home.

Still, she did not dare to look directly at her family for more than a moment at a time. The reality of how far away they would be from now on pierced her heart. Her farewell to each of them had transpired before she was in the public eye. From the time her hand was given in marriage, she communicated only unspoken phrases with her penetrating gaze. Her parents understood and kept themselves together until they were in private. None could betray the sorrow and grief they were experiencing. As parents they felt they had put their child on the altar of a foreign god.

Mara felt the gentle weight of the golden key, hidden beneath her garments, reminding her of their love, and of Aunt Olivera, who had gone this way before. In contrast to the cold *kaşbastı*, this key had come to her warm, and remained constant. It gave her courage to think of it now.

Although she ate little that night, she anchored her heart into the promises of God, and as she prayed, she sensed Holy Spirit close at hand. In her mind's eye she saw herself entering through a large iron gate that clanged behind her, but the sense of God's Presence smiled at her side, and she knew she was not alone.

And so Mara smiled that smile forward, first at her new mother-in-law, then to the women around her. She gathered a few of the rose petals she had been blessed with in one hand, and blew them to the girls who circled her in dance. She knew who she was and to Whom she belonged. Her courtesy to each person in the Sultan's family was genuine. She chose to embrace her new life and love those around her. By the time the carriages left for Bursa, the ice in the Sultan's mother's eyes and tone had subsided. Instead she had become patronizing and protective. Mara wasn't sure which was more challenging.

Abdiya Wesab

Part II:

The Harem

Mara entered the Harem as one might enter a kingdom set apart. As the doors closed behind her the clang was not simply metal on metal. The reverberation silenced the world outside. The silence was not present inside the great walls. It was a world of its own, full of sounds. A pace of its own, full of expectations. A future of its own full of uncertainties. A caste system of its own, full of potential pitfalls. A chess match of its own, played by dainty hands with steeled wills.

Mara was led through narrow corridors into a central courtyard, which seemed to her the heart of the square complex which faced towards itself. Every room looked upon the marble fountain centered in this tiled space. Sky was ceiling here. Intricately carved railings framed various outdoor staircases which curved their ways up to the second floor, which was unified with a balcony. The complex felt more a miniature village than a building. Back through the various corridors Mara was later to discover the many other domed buildings which hugged the outside of this main sanctuary. These, she would find, housed the kitchens and laundries, pantries and infirmary, the tailor and upholsterer, the stables and butcher.

Mara entered the Harem with the quiet, intention to carry Peace, and the purposeful intention to carry the heart of Father God behind these bars to women and children who would shape the future.

The Harem and the seat of the Sultan were based in the capitol of the Ottoman Empire, in the city of Bursa. Mara knew that this had also been the ancient capitol of the Roman Empire, in the time before Constantine, when there were four Emperors sharing the responsibilities of the huge domain. It felt curious to be in a city with so much history, and be just one small person longing for God's Peace to transform the region.

Abdiya Wesab

Mara's room was gained through two wooden doors, maintained by a large key she was entrusted with. It was an ample room, housed sparsely with a wide couch, low brazier, small carved table, and wall sconce. Two large arched windows faced the fountain in the courtyard. From these limpid light accessed one half of the room. In the recesses the many cushioned couch remained restfully in shadows. Wall hangings kept the damp at bay, the rugs underfoot rustled softly with the customary fragrant herbs tucked beneath.

Mara felt the room became her. As the eunuch deposited her chest near the couch, she breathed deeply. Nodding her thanks as he shut the door behind her, she rested in the Peace she carried. Kneeling at the edge of the couch she gave thanks to the Lord for bringing her this far, and asked for His Presence to remain. Quietly, she touched the door posts and lintel with anointing oil and blessed the space, inviting Him in[24].

On her first day in the Harem, Mara learned how intentionally life was specifically inside, as befit the role of women in Islam. She was taught that the Harem was a sacred, inviolable apartment where only female members, children, and eunuch slaves of the family were allowed. Because Islam taught that women held nine parts of the desires given to mankind, they needed to be kept away from men, for they would otherwise lead them astray[25]. As Mara was shown around the complex, she was told that keeping women covered in public assured good Muslim women that their husbands would never be led astray by other women who were not properly attired.

"This also protects us from advances from strange men," Mara was told. "Besides, not being able to be seen allows us privacy, and highlights our character, rather than our physical traits."

Mara studied her mother-in-law as she talked. She was the Mehd-i-ulya[26], or 'Cradle of the Great'. She alone had borne this Sultan, and thereby gained the right to be the ruler of the women's quarters. As Mara had heard on the long carriage ride to Bursa, this lady was a Dulkadirid princess.

The Dulkadirid were a mighty people who ruled more territory than the Sultan himself. Across Asia their influence ran to the rising sun in Mosul on their frontier to the east. At least, this was what Emine Hâtûn said. She had been the first princess to marry a Sultan, bringing, as Mara did, a political union to establish peace. Emine Hâtûn, Mehd-i-ulya, as one properly addressed her highness, received obeisance from all the women in the Harem. This palace was her turf. Her carriage was regal, she the supreme ruler of the Harem. Mara gave her full attention. This matriarch was the Queen here, and was to be obeyed at any cost.

"This is especially pertinent on Fridays or *Cuma,* the day of Muslim prayer!"

Emine Hâtûn raised her eyebrows, "or at any of the five times a day that the people are called to the duty of praying to Allah."

Emine Hâtûn's robes swished on the stone pavements as she walked, pushing curtains aside to show Mara where she might go, and pointing to doors that were forbidden. Along each wall, alcoves with incense flickered, casting shadows. The scent was carries by light summer breezes from corridor to courtyard, and mingled with the natural smells of life it was seeking to mask.

Mara was glad it was summer. The courtyard was enjoyable, and kept fresh with bouquets and blooming trees. Like a miniature replica of the out of doors, its gently splashing fountains invited even bees and birds across the high walls, while keeping others out.

"You will assist in maintaining this area," Emine Hâtûn was saying. Mara focused carefully on her instructions. "The wives have various children. Picking up after them, and assuring the Sultan that his arrival at any moment would be welcome and celebrated is an important role for a newly arriving wife. It will acquaint you with the ebb and flow of life here, and make you familiar with the daily calendar."

They moved on past the rooms of the women into the outer courts. A tailor was at work in one sunny room, younger women were washing laundry in another.

Great steaming cauldrons bubbled with bedding. Several were pounding this, while others pumped a steady stream of water into the rinsing trough. In other rooms various tasks were being achieved by what seemed a sea of slaves. Oil lamps were being cleaned, candles made, the thick divan pillows were being opened, beaten, cleaned and sewn back together, rugs were being mended. It was a beehive of activity.

"That reminds me of your wardrobe, child," Emine Hâtûn said, turning Mara towards herself unceremoniously to inspect her. She adjusted Mara's belt a little higher and stepped back to scrutinize her.

"You've been wearing your *cevberi* too low," she explained, "it needs to be high, so that all the folds can gather beneath it and show off the skirts to flow uninterrupted. But, let me see," she turned Mara around to see her from all sides.

The *cevberi* belt was another one of the wardrobe additions which had come with the marriage. It was elaborate, and hooked in front. Mara's was in the shape of a leaf, which she liked. It reminded her of the out of doors. Mehd-i-ulya's was two hooked circles. She had seen some women with jeweled daggers, and others with birds. It seemed to be a statement that described a person. The *cevberi* were useful as well. It gave one a place to hook one's purse to. Mara had been given an embroidered velvet key purse as her welcome to the Harem. It allowed her to lock her own little room.

Long before leaving home, Mara's aunt Olivera had helped her sew her own apparel, suited as it must be, to the Ottoman court. They had chosen the homegrown woven linen for summer and wool for winter from the fields of home. Carefully stitching fresh chemise to wear next to her skin and the traditional *şalvar* trousers she would be wearing under her frock was the first step. They had kept these simple and in natural hues, so as to blend in with whatever wardrobe adjustments might be made by the court. They had made several shifts to wear over the chemise, and long kirtles of plain dark colors to wear over those. Her fitted kirtles had full skirts with added triangles. The sleeves were fitted to the wrist, with a taper down to her knuckles.

Olivera had taught her how to crochet and then embroider around the edges of cloth. "These will be your veils, dear," she had explained, "they are mostly only worn outside the house, but are always handy so you can pull them quickly up around your face if a man comes in."

"I can't be sure these will still be acceptable wear in the modern Ottoman court," Aunt Olivera had smiled, almost apologetically, "it has been quite some time since I was there, and even then, it was a time of turmoil and war when I left."

Mara remembered all this as she curtsied appropriately to Mehd-i-ulya, showing in her behavior that she was submitting to whatever was dictated.

"Your *kaftans* are too simple, and we need to add color contrasts. You look like an old woman," Emine Hâtûn smiled patronizingly, "you have a lot of competition here, amongst all these beautiful wives and women. You need to be the political wife who produces a son, so you can follow in my footsteps."

Submitting to Emine Hâtûn's firm grip, Mara was soon in the tailor's room. She was met by a curious mixture of mysterious spices, beeswax, and the dust of a veritable mountain of silks. She stifled a sneeze. An old eunuch looked up and then stood quickly to show obeisance to Mehd-i-ulya.

"Our newest wife, Abdul!" Emine Hâtûn shoved Mara into the center of the room. "She needs more color in her kaftans. And let's add a *bürümcük* between the lower kaftan and the *şalvar*."

"Do you embroider, child?" she asked Mara.

"Yes, Mehd-i-ulya Hanim." Mara replied politely, wondering where this was going.

Emine Hâtûn clapped her hands twice. "That's decided then. She can keep the inner kaftan, but embroider it with needle lace around the throat." Here she lifted the edge of Mara's kirtle at the neck to see if she had a hem suitable for lace. In so doing she saw the chain around Mara's neck.

"What is this?" she asked, pulling it out.

"It is a necklace my aunt gave me as a farewell gift," Mara said, "Her name was Despina Hâtûn, wife of Beyazid."

"Is that so?" Emine Hâtûn said, scrutinizing the key, "it's very unique."

"Yes," Mara said, beginning to feel uncomfortable. She hoped wearing a necklace wasn't a problem.

"Very kind of your aunt to be so generous with you," Emine Hâtûn said, then, changing the subject abruptly, turned back to Abdul, "Please show us silks that we can use to create an appropriate *bürümcük* to wear over that."

The tailor obligingly lifted rolls of silks from a corner and began spreading them across the table with a flourish. Mara would have been content with the first, but Hâtûn insisted on holding each one up to her skin, at the window. It soon became clear that a *bürümcük* was a crepe overskirt and bodice with sleeves.

"These three, Abdul!" Emine Hâtûn ordered, snapping her fingers. A striped silk woven in various greens that included a thin band of crimson was to be prepared first. The flowered silk in shades of blue was to be done by next week, and a large print in russet, walnut and umber was to be completed by the end of the month.

"Her *iç entari* is to be matched with sleeves like these of her current kaftan, but done to wear under the inner robes. Mara, you are to shorten the sleeves of this kaftan so that the *bürümcük* shows from underneath. Abdul, see to it that it has a   deep and low neckline. Her embroidery is to show from below." The tailor bowed in agreement.

"Mara, you have a sufficient *ferace*, but it will only do for summer, and is really only needed if we have outings. But Abdul, she is to be prepared for winter as you know we have it here. Show us what you have."

Mara was already overwhelmed with the rich assortments and quick transition of her garments. She quickly gathered that a *ferace* was her outer kirtle, seeing as this was the only garment Emine Hâtûn had not discussed yet.

Abdul deftly shoved the mountain of summer silks to one side and procured a stack of heavier weave. Mara soon learned that the *kemha* was brocade, the velvet *kadife*, and when metallic threads were added the cloth became *seraser*. It was beautiful, and her respect for the quality and submission to Emine Hâtûn's ministrations had softened the older woman's reserve a little more.

"Abdul, when you complete these winter kaftan's you are to compliment them with furs to color, you understand?" Emine Hâtûn ordered. He bowed. "Mara, do you prefer sable, marten or ermine?"

It was the first time Mara's opinion had been asked on anything. She instantly knew it was a test. She curtsied. "I trust your judgment, Mehd-i-ulya Hanim."

The tours and instructions continued for weeks. Emine Hâtûn had a new inmate to introduce to seraglio living, and Mara knew it was wisdom to learn all she was taught. All Muslim men kept their wives and concubines in *haremlik* - in separate chambers or parts of their tent or dwelling, she found out. This left the *selamlik* - or the place where men met and came and went freely, open and without the distraction of the female. But a Sultan ruled, and so his harem was in a special enclosure or *seraglio*, It had many layers of administration, managed, as Mara was frequently reminded, by the Sultan's mother. Discipline, choices of new concubines, which new arrivals should be slaves, and what was purchased all passed under Mehd-i-ulya's watchful eye and keen decision making.

Sweeping was usually reserved for the lower class wives or servants, but Mara loved to sweep when no one was around. She hummed childhood songs, and remembered the footsteps of the dances that went with them. Today she

Abdiya Wesab

was sweeping the long hall that led to the
kitchen area.

Sing first, sister of brother!
Drag your song, bend your song!
Bring your song as you did it
while you lived with your brothers.

I used to ascend a hill,
I used to descend in a valley
A white bird-cherry blossoms
On the hill
A swift river flows in the valley

I ascend the hill to adorn myself
I descend in the valley to wash myself
Sing first, sister of brother!
Dance with your song,
Bend to the notes[27].

Mara hummed quietly, singing bits in her mother tongue. The Harem's sub-structure within a vast kingdom felt inhibiting to Mara. She had loved the freedom of being outside, alone, able to choose where she went and what she did. Increasingly this sense of confinement made her feel almost choked. She knew it wasn't sufficient to find release in dance or sweeping, she needed the Holy Spirit's help.

So she took the issue to the Lord, and asked for His empowering. She sensed his Peace come afresh, and felt Him speak to her heart. She was His Light here, and to do so, she must come in respectfully and humbly, through the door these other women did. "But small is the gate and narrow the way that leads to life, and only a few find it.[28]" she heard in her spirit. Yes, good Scripture to apply here, to her situation.

It was a sacrifice to give up the vastness of God's creation and be watched and directed, overseen and evaluated. It was even harder to live constantly with a group of women who hadn't yet made room in their hearts for Jesus. But He was with her, and would lead forward. And it was not forever. Comforted, she paid closer attention, and realigned her heart's attitude. She felt for the key around her neck and held it for a moment. It reminded her of home, warming her heart.

Suddenly she remembered a day in her childhood. Her brothers were outside, playing at horseback riding and jousting in the courtyard. She was in the window, upstairs, looking down. Her mother had come up behind her and they had watched together, smiling at the rowdy bunch. Mother had started quoting words from a hymn, "Oh Bridle of racing young horses, wing of soaring birds, safe rudder of sailing boats, shepherd of the royal lambs ...[29]"

"Brother Christ, I need you to be my bridle, my Savior, my "plowing shepherd, my steering helmsman, my heavenly pinion. Pull me to a life of sweetness and joy, a sheep gathered by Thy Spirit!" she continued the hymn, "Footsteps of Christ, aeon which never ends" lead me, so that I can face this "bridle" and submit willingly to the Narrow Path you have chosen for me!"

Mara learned the pecking order. She was a political wife. This placed her at the head of the line, without having to go through all the hoops that other foreign women did. Normally, those who came into the harem came as war booty, or tithed slaves, chosen for exceptional beauty. These only rose in rank to become a *Gözde* or Noticed Favorite if they pleased the Sultan when they shared his bed. And they only got offered that chance if and when Mehd-i-ulya looked them over, sorted them out, and decided they qualified.

From the beginning Muhammed the Prophet's followers had strict rules dictating that when men went out and raided, they could keep the women and children for themselves as war booty, however twenty percent was given to Muhammed as a type of tithe or tax[30].

The Sultan had come to replace the one that men tithed to, as representative of the Sword of Islam. Many women were tithed to the harem. Most of them were simply there to be put through a training in etiquette so that the Sultan would have a woman to give as a reward to build the harems of his best serving men. A woman given by the Sultan was the highest badge of honor a man could receive. Thus the standards set in the Sultan's harem were constantly being reevaluated and sharpened.

If a women was chosen to stay in the harem for the Sultan, and pleased him as *Gözde,* she entered a waiting list, and served the Sultan in many little ways, always within view, as the term *Gözde* literally meant. If she caught his attention again she moved up in rank to being *Ikbal* or The Fortunate. Now she might spend more time in his presence, and depending on circumstances, his choices, and if he was busy at war, or home resting, he might choose her. If she should produce offspring, the child was considered potential royalty. Potential because the child had to receive the final word and approval of the Sultan himself.

Having sons was problematic because the Sultan's oldest son was his heir. Yet, in a culture of so much war and politics, history had shown that some sons died fighting, and others had recently died at their father's decision. Murad had himself fought an eleven year civil war with his four brothers who threatened his throne[31]. His grandfather, for whom he was named, had been threatened by three of his own sons: Ibrahim, Halil and Savci[32]. Each of these had been killed by their father for this threat, making the role of son much more tentative in the eyes of a present day Sultan.

Mara was informed that she herself was a *Kadın* which meant 'the Woman or Wife'. A Sultan kept four such wives at a time. If one died, or he divorced a *Kadın*, her space was filled with another political marriage, or with one of the *Ikbal* who had borne a son. Currently, she was the fourth wife. This put her in a position to be present in his inner circle, speak when spoken to, travel with him should he invite the *Kadın*, and be in direct relationship with the Sultan's mother. She was not responsible to produce a son, or be present with him at all times. As consort, she answered directly and only to Mehd-i-ulya.

Mara was sitting by a window, dutifully doing the embroidery she had been assigned to do. It was not unpleasant work, and it afforded her the chance to gaze out on the walled garden while listening to the women around her. It was curious how Emine Hâtûn had softened over the last few weeks. Mara understood that she clung desperately to the importance of her role as Empress Mother. She was the gatekeeper and ruler of the Harem. Hers was the highest position. Listening to her, and watching her interactions Mara felt the insecurities that kept her role more militant than motherly.

Emine Hâtûn was going over the schedule for the baths with the newest girls, some of whom seemed overwhelmed. One fidgeted with the tassels on the edge of her kirtle, another chewed her nails. Mara's heart went out to them. With a glance she gathered that they were all from the slave market. A translator was making sure each girl understood what she was being told. The list of things to do correctly was long.

Mara remembered stifling a giggle when she was told that they had to enter the washroom with the left foot first. But then she had learned the protocol got even more exacting with hand washing.

Mara smiled. It felt good to not be the newest girl any more and have some milestones to look back on. The fact that she wasn't learning one more thing, but established, and sitting with work in hand, knowing what was expected of her was progress.

Deftly creating picot on the edge of her project, Mara began the satin stitch floral pattern. She had been quick to learn that all decorative work must be geometric or floral and never include the replication of an animal or human.

Birds, however, were exceptions, especially if a tree of life was being created. A flash of wings outside the window caught her attention. A pair of redstarts flitting about, chatting gaily and cocking their heads made her smile. Curious and friendly, they ignored her presence and went about their business of foraging. Mara wondered how much work it would be to incorporate a design of feathers into her handiwork.

The training circle under Emine Hâtûn's tutelage moved on, feet in mincing step, satin dresses swishing ever so softly, as became them. Having that many women to oversee must be overwhelming, Mara thought, yet Mehd-i-ulya seemed to be in her element.

Mara remembered that her Aunt Olivera had been a Sultan's wife before Emine. Yet how differently their lives had taken shape! But that was due to many factors. Emine had born the daughter of a rival Sultan, Olivera was the daughter of a ruler several kingdoms away. Emine had gladly taken the helm, Olivera knew her role was to love those around her and bring peace. Mara was thankful to have her example to turn back to again and again.

Several of the mother's came into the courtyard, with their children. Mara got up to join them. It was pleasant by the fountain. The sun had come around and was filling the patio with light. Bees and birds found their way over the tall walls and second story roof down into this little sanctuary.

One of the little girls ran up to let the fountain spray water on her face, laughing. Her playmate skipped over to join her. Mara picked blossoms from the flowers growing in clay pots around the couches nearby and used her embroidery floss to weave garlands for the girls. Laughing, they put on their crowns and danced together. Their laughter carried down the corridors of the Harem, carrying joy and smiles. Women stopped what they were doing and came to their doorways to watch the girls.

Because of the nature of suspicion cast most recently over the sons of the Sultans, Mara prayed that she would not have a son. They were expected to rule and aspired to be Sultan. The mothers of the Sultan's older sons were already haughty and watched each other with suspicion. Mothers of daughters were treated differently.

Mara clapped her hands for the dancers. These littlest daughters of the Sultan were so much fun to be with. They gravitated to her. Perhaps it was because she always had a game, rhyme or song to share with them. Digging in her sewing basket, she reached below her current work and got out the handkerchiefs prepared for embroidery. She took one up and folded it deftly into a little doll, handing it to one of the girls. Her delight drew the others in, and soon each child had one.

Being here, and listening to the conversations around her, Mara had learned that princesses are called *Schezade*. Whereas a normal woman could expect to be in the harem of a man, no matter her status in life, the daughter of a Sultan was a *Schezade*. When a marriage was arranged for her, the son-in-law was called *Damat*, and could only take this one wife, to honor her connection to the Sultan. She was given an estate, and the Damat served her, and the family house.

'Perhaps that's why mothers of daughters seem more peaceful?' Mara thought. *'There are so many strata to the culture of the Harem. Most of the women are focused on climbing the social ladder for status. But perhaps this is because it's the natural expectation here? It is the tone set by Mehd-i-ulya. She does not mean*

ill. She is trying to keep this little kingdom running smoothly. But the women are tense. Lord, show me how to carry Your Holy Spirit well in this environment.'

Mara found that being willing to jump up and do as she was asked was one of the best responses. She had no complaint or expectation to achieve rank. She simply was a friends. She also asked each of the women to do all that they could to teach her Ottoman Turkish. She laughed easily at herself, and didn't take offense when they corrected her. Several of the other women had also come from Europe and were also still learning. It was an ongoing process and they were glad to have someone newer than themselves to be able to teach.

Spring was well advanced when Emine Hâtûn decided that it was time for all the *Kadın* to embroider a cloth to cover the grave of her deceased husband, the former Sultan. It was a good use of a rain-spattered, cloud-filled day. The women gathered near a brazier and held the cloth over their knees, careful to not pull it away from each other.

Mara was thankful that in the time she had been here, Emine Hâtûn had warmed to her. She was beginning to sense inclusion with the other women too. It was a good feeling. While they worked, Mara asked Emine Hâtûn about her homeland and her eyes got soft. "I come from the Cradle of Civilization," she said, "a land of rolling hills, a vast steppe, that leads down to the Euphrates

River. As you know, my father's father's father's family are Dulkadirs. Our city is Elbistan. Can you guess what grows best in our region?" Her eyes smiled, inviting the *Kadın* into a game.

"Maybe sheep?" Mara ventured.

When Emine Hâtûn shook her head. "Wheat?"

"Grapes?" Halime ventured. Halime was one of the senior wives, home for a few weeks.

Emine Hâtûn laughed. "No, its orchid roots! The *sahlep* we serve comes from our very own district," she said proudly. "We harvest and dry the roots, then we grind them to make the milky, hot *sahlep* to drink. Do you like it?"

Mara nodded. She was enjoying all the different menus which she was being introduced to. "I'm loving the food here, Mehd-i-ulya Hanım," she said. "I think my favorite so far is your rice with raisins, saffron, and toasted pine nuts!"

Halime patted her on the leg. "Yes, you need to fatten up a bit, my dear. Eat well. The Sultan notices his well endowed wives."

Mara quietly changed the subject. "Really, Mehd-i-ulya Hanım, your kitchen is probably the best on earth. I don't know how you manage. You not only have to over see the kitchen, garden, and grounds. You have such a mother's heart for the Sultan. I think that without you he would not be so strong."

Emine Hâtûn's eyes moistened. Mara suddenly realized that few noticed her for who she was. "You know," she said, "you and I are very much alike. We are both political brides. Sultan Mehmed, my husband, made an important alliance with our Dulkadir confederation by marrying me. We have always been rich in horses and horsemen. Even King Solomon came to us for horses! It was my fortune to become the mother of Murad II. May you also be blessed with good fortune, my daughter."

"Thank you, Mehd-i-ulya Hanım. I feel fortunate just being here. I am happy that there is peace in my father's land, and I am making new friends. And I love the children. It's nice having so many little ones around. They replace my little brother and sister."

Emine motioned to a slave girl to light another lamp. It was difficult to see the embroidery work. "Yes," she said, "I was just the same. The harem has become my home. I'm glad it's full of children!"

"And Bursa really is - how do you call it - *Hüdavendigar*!" Mara added, trying one of the new words she was learning in Turkish. "When I look outside and see the mountain, and breathe such fresh air, I am reminded it is 'God's gift'.

The *Kadın* smiled and nodded.

"Good for you!" Halime said, "you're learning fast!"

"And you've only been here a while! Just wait! Peaches come ripe soon. That's heaven, for sure!" another wife called Hüma said.

"Peaches! Ah yes!" Emine Hâtûn smiled, "perhaps the queen of Bursa's delights!"

"And during Ramadan, the *Karagöz and Hacivat* shadow players will come around and entertain us!" added Yeni Hâtûn, who was yet another *Kadın,* "you will like it!"

Mara Hâtûn

Whenever I see those jokers I think of the songs of my childhood!" Halime said.

Sing us one, Halime Hatun!" Hüma said, clapping.

Halime got up and began singing, swaying to the song with the rhythm of her homeland,

"Wrangling running horses,
We are catching them!
Stretching, running together,
My noble steeds! Waiting to be friends.
Horses gallop past,
These my noble steeds!
Waiting to be friends.
From a bright steep rocky mountain
Hurrying they descend

Abdiya Wesab

They whinny as they journey
Into the mountain river
Crossing over, horses
These my noble steeds
Waiting to be friends[33]."

Several other women had stopped to look in on the sewing party, hearing the singing. They all clapped.

"Well done, Halime Hâtûn!" Mehd-i-ulya declared. "Just see how splendid we are here," she continued, waving at the women assembled to listen to the song, "ladies gathered from across the world, in one family! Perhaps this evening at supper several others would like to regal us with songs from home? That was delightful, Halime Hâtûn!"

Mara Ḥâtûn

Halime curtseyed and received the aplomb with graciousness. She embodied royalty much as Emine Hâtûn did. Mara wondered about her heritage. She was so regal!

As the women returned to their various tasks Mehd-i-ulya went on, "Yes, we abound in delights in Bursa," she began, then she clapped her hands decisively. "You know, Mara, I think you've been here several weeks already and you've not seen Bursa. Tomorrow the *Kadın* will go for a tour in a carriage. You should see the silk market and how it is woven. We might even be able to find a few early peaches!"

True to her word, the four wives and Emine Hâtûn piled into a generous, cushioned carriage the next day. Emine placed Mara next to a window and they all pointed out highlights as they drove through the city. Mara was next to Halime Hâtûn. Mara had learned she was proud mother of two grown sons. She was a beautiful woman with a vivacious character. She loved to laugh and joke. Mara knew she was actually only in Bursa for the summer. Usually she lived with her younger son, as was customary. Sons grew up and were entrusted to Masters, to learn administration. Halime's sons Ahmed and Alaeddin were learning to rule and prove themselves to their father. This was done in a different province to test their loyalty. If the supervisor felt they did well, the Sultan was pleased. Currently, he was pleased.

Mara Hâtûn

Across from Mara was Hüma Hâtûn, who was fast becoming a friend. They were both from Europe, and shared culture. They also seemed to have the same personality. Hüma had no ambition to be the First Wife, or rule. She was more intent on making sure the children played well together and had happy memories. Her son was three years old and very nearly Mara's favorite child. Hüma was about Mara's age, and had come into the Harem as a slave girl. She just happened to catch the Sultan's eye, and now was a *Kadın*, almost by accident. She had no airs, and Mara liked her.

Emine Hâtûn sat between her and Yeni Hâtûn, another wife. She was a quiet young woman with sad eyes. Emine seemed kind enough to her. Mara wondered what the trouble was.

But she didn't have long to ponder life inside the carriage. The wonderful milieu of street life surrounded them the moment the carriage left the palace grounds. Street vendors nearly tripped on each other seeking to gain the attention of the inhabitants of their vehicle. Men with great poles across their shoulders had leather buckets from which they dished slabs of sliced yogurt. Hunters still in their hooded capes touted rings of curlew and thrush, partridge and plover. Mara turned her head away. She didn't care to see dead birds. She loved them flying and alive.

"Buy my strings of onions and garlics," a farmer just ahead was shouting. Next to him a boy was nearly hidden in brooms which were laden on his shoulders. "Buy my brooms! I've a large one for the ladies and a small one for the babies, buy my brooms,[34]" his plaintive voice sang out. Mara saw a ribbon vendor with a tall hat out of the corner of her eye, bright sashes blowing in the spring breeze as they turned a corner. They all wore the clogs of spring, she noticed. Shoes with extra long wooden heels so as to not become tangled in the mud underfoot.

"Fresh fish, caught in the Marmara, delivered to your door," came the call from an old man with a flat basket of fish balanced on his head. His wide shoulders were wet with the dripping meat. Mara could just imagine the smell he would bear home by nightfall! "Lemons for salad, lemons for salad!" a boy darts between the men. Nearby a man was dishing out beakers of leeches for medical cures. She shuddered watching the black creatures slither about in the water. "Yorganji!" a ruddy faced old man shouts, throwing his voice to echo it off the buildings. Mara smiled. She was proud to have learned that 'yorgan' means quilt.

The Lanier, with his back-basket full of wool, and a nearby milliner had more more appealing wares. Tinkers and knife sharpens were beating out rhythms, metal on stone, and singing along, trying to capture customers. Cakes and pastries floated by on the head of a child, while firewood, turnip, and sweet rush vendors offered their wares. Boys selling birdcages woven ingeniously of brush, and a jovial old man with hand carved wooden spoons rumbled past them outside the window.

Before Mara knew it, Emine Hâtûn had already told the driver to stop. He tied up the horses and entered a nearby shop. Mara took in the sea of pedestrians who were being beaten back by guards, to ensure that the royal carriage had plenty of berth. Women and children scattered quickly, knowing that these guards were fierce and had a reputation to live up to. The market was a boisterous affair, and Mara wished she could step out of the carriage herself and take in the sounds and smells. Tantalizing hints of flavor crept in the cracks, attesting to the presence of a bakery nearby. A gypsy cart ambled past, stacked high with fragrant rose blossoms. Another cart of fruit stacked higher than she thought possible rumbled by. Before she knew it, the servant was back with a heaping mound of what looked like snow. Mara wondered if it would melt as he passed it in to them.

"This is *Pişmaniye.*" Emine Hâtûn announced proudly, "you must taste some Mara!" Up close it looked like spun silk, in a ball.

"Is it silk, Mehd-i-ulya Hanım?" she asked.

Emine Hâtûn laughed. "No. This is a delight made by roasting flour and sugar in butter and then spinning it into candy. But it does look like silk, doesn't it girls?"

Everyone was delicately helping themselves to the fresh candy. "It's one of those things one wants to eat fresh." Halime commented, "when it's stale it takes on a totally different nature."

"Don't eat too much, though," Emine Hâtûn cautioned, "we will be nibbling our way around the city, and that sugar can make you thirsty."

"Too late!" laughed Halime, licking her fingers.

Mara stopped herself from taking another bite. Thirst was not a pleasant thing to imagine.

The silk worm farm and its vast mulberry orchard was not what she had imagined. At last they might climb out of the carriage and personally touch and see the operation. Once the concept of tiny worms chewing leaves and spinning was explained to her she fancied she could hear them chewing. Inside, the silks were being painted with *Ebru*. Artists placed oil paint on water, stirred it into a pattern, then laid the silk on top. Each piece came out differently. It was so beautiful!

Then they went to the peach orchard. The aroma was intoxicating. Mara almost wept to gaze upon trees as far as the eye could see. They took tea in the shade of the heavy fruit and were given several boxes to bring home with them. Mara would have liked to have stayed and help harvest. It reminded her of home.

Before long the sun started sliding down the horizon and they needed to head back. "Maybe another day we should go up to the snow line on the mountain." Emine Hâtûn said as they got back in the carriage.

"That would be truly amazing!" Mara said dreamily. It had been a lovely day. She was starting to feel more at ease. Mara had enjoyed being outside most of all. To look freely at the mountain without a lattice, to breathe fresh air, and stroll in sunshine refreshed her.

Ramadan came around on the calendar and Emine Hâtûn explained that for a lunar month the entire household would fast during the day, and eat at night. "Ramadan is a time of obligatory fasting for the entire Empire," she explained. "It is a time for us to practice self-discipline, cleanse our souls of impurities, and practice charity. We want our good deeds to outweigh any thing we may have done wrong. Good deeds earn us *thawab* or spiritual rewards. These are multiplied during Ramadan. For this reason, we also will have more *salat* or prayer times and the entire Quran will be recited by the palace *imam* or priest."

Mara Hâtûn

Emine Hâtûn knew that Mara was a Christian. Early on she had respectfully explained that she had chosen to stay a Follower of Jesus, but that she would participate in all that Emine Hâtûn asked her to unless she felt God asking her not to. Emine Hâtûn had looked at her sharply and acknowledged that she had heard this request.

Mara talked with God about Ramadan. She felt Him encouraging her to take part with the rest of the household this year, and model Peace and the simple Joy of being forgiven. She knew there was no weighing out of good deeds over bad ones. She joined the fast to show respect to the household. Jesus had already done the only Deed that could bring salvation from sins by dying on the Cross.

Abdiya Wesab

So she joined in the festive work, helping to prepare extra food for guests, serving it through the night. She assisted the mothers with their children. There were several who were pregnant or nursing. These were to eat regularly. She helped to make sure their food was delivered to them. She took part in the fast, and ate with the family at night, when they had *Iftar*, the evening meal which broke the fast. She went to prayer when the family did; whispering her prayers to the Lord of Heaven and Earth; talking with Jesus, and feeling Holy Spirit close at hand, with her. When they went to the mosque to listen to the *imam* recite the Quran, she offered to stay at home with the small children. She had already been chosen as their favorite, so it was a mutual pleasure.

Several evenings the *Karagöz and Hacivat* shadow players came and did puppet plays for the whole household. These were the latest tradition in Ramadan entertainment. Apparently a common man had wanted to convey something to the last Sultan. Not wanting to offend anyone outright, he had told the story using puppets. The Sultan was so impressed that he brought the case to justice and hired the man.

Karagöz and *Hacivat* were the two main characters in the shadow play. One of them representing the aloof, wealthy and educated, the other looking at the world from a much lower perspective. Mara was still working on her Turkish, but she understood enough to see why everyone was laughing. The first scene opened with a song and prayer. Then the plot would unfold, build, and end with an argument where *Hacivat* told *Karagöz* that he had ruined everything. *Karagöz* seemed to end each performance saying "May my transgressions be forgiven."

Mara found that thought provoking. She longed to tell everyone that their sins could be forgiven. But she had not yet felt an openness to share her full heart in a way that would be understood. As she did every day, she prayed that God would show her when it was time, and who was ready to hear Truth. As she did she reached up and held the key for a moment, almost like an anchor.

During Ramadan there was more coming and going, and there were many more mouths to feed. Halime Hâtûn and her sons came. Halime mother, who was also the Sultan's sister, and Halime's brother came. His wives were also half sisters to the Sultan. Yeni Hâtûn's family was meant to come, but a storm had formed across Anatolia, forcing them to turn back. Mara felt sorry for her. She had never yet seen her smile.

Charity was also an important part of Ramadan. Mara found opportunity to help in the kitchen and pack food to be given away to those who had none. She enjoyed that. Mornings had always been her favorite time of day. She soon found that she could help prepare and serve *Suhur*, the pre-fast meal, which was the last meal served while it is still dark, before dawn and the day long fast. She loved being up before the sun, breathing in the deep, cool stillness of starlight, and the fast of silence creation took.

Working in the kitchen and serving the other wives was only typical of how Mara had served at her mother's side back at home. To her it was a natural aspect of being royalty. One served well. In this way she found Ramadan to be a highlight of her season at the palace to date.

Mara hummed to herself as she cut up the apples, dates and apricots for supper,

"My dear, get up early wash clean,
Take the keys, go out into the fields.
Oh Lord, unlock the earth
Unleash the dew,

The honeyed dew, unleash the grass
The silken grass[35]."

Halime Hâtûn had been back to her son's side for several months, but she was with them at the Harem for Ramadan. Mara welcomed her with a warm smile, remembering the ride in the countryside, the peach orchard, and the delightful tour of Bursa's silk.

Halime looked right past her, however, perhaps not recognizing her or assuming that she was a mere *Gözde*. Mara followed her gaze. She was watching the Sultan with a curious intensity. Mara wondered what was going on for a moment, then became too busy serving to remain focused on their interaction. She had also seen so many exchanges between the women and the Sultan that she had very nearly tired of their ways.

When they wanted something it seemed that coy persuasions were the required or expected ways to get it from him. Because he was the only one with power to give them what they wanted, he, in turn very nearly could have drowned in the affections of so many devoted wives and concubines. Knowing, however, that their affections were for personal gain, he viewed them as transactions, as was only reasonable from his perspective. Besides, in pleasing the one woman, he could easily displease a host of others. Therefore his relationships with them were handled with caution; his royal self must be protected from being caught in the crossfire of female spats.

Halime, however, was the most persistent. When she wanted something, she usually got it. Having such an intertwined relationship with her family was a delicate business. If he failed to deliver, or to impress upon her how important it was to her betterment that he did not deliver, the subject would come back to haunt him through his sister, Halime's mother, or through his brother-in-law, or his half sisters who were married to them. It could very nearly drive a man to distraction. Although she was beautiful, it was almost a relief that she was usually away with Alaeddin Ali, serving him as he learned to rule. Therefore her glances did not go unnoticed. The Sultan knew better than to ignore her.

It seemed to Mara as if she had just begun to get used to being awake most of the night when Ramadan was over, and the *Eid al-Fitr* holiday began. This festive occasion was filled with food during the day, and more entertainment. Sugar and candies, delicacies and pastries were served almost continually. Hundreds of people came to honor the Sultan. Special music and new clothing were part of the event as well. Mara wondered how many months it took to get ready for something this spectacular.

Again, she found being with the children the most life-giving. How genuine and free children are! Little

Mehmed was enthralled with the puppeteers. The little girls were excited to dance about in new costumes. But when it was all over and life settled back to normal again, Mara was relieved.

It also felt like a season had shifted for her personally. She could speak fairly clearly with the women around her now, and had earned their trust. Yes, for any who asked or observed her closely, it was clear that she was not a Muslim. But she served without expecting anything in return. She was pleasant to be around. She didn't hold grudges or try and use her female powers to get anything. She just lived forgiven and simply confident in who she was in Jesus, and this blessed the people around her without them even knowing why.

Abdiya Wesab

Sun hit the little lemon tree in the courtyard by the fountain for about an hour a day as winter came. Mara loved the dappled light that played in her room as a result. Recent letters from home lay in her lap. She played with the key around her neck as she read. Katerina wrote about how she and Ulrich were doing in Celje. She very much wanted children, and hadn't had any yet. Lazar wasn't given much to writing, but from what she heard from her parents, he was dedicated to the land and their people. Stefan was also reported to be involved in strengthening walls and moats, and the planting of trees to replace those lost in the various raids of the last ten years. Grgur was happily married and his wife Jelisaveta had given birth to a son. They named him Vuk after their grandfather.

Mara Ḫâtûn

Mara took up her quill and wrote:

This week the ladies of the harem went to a thermal spring here in Bursa. It was a larger outing than I imagined, for everyone went. All the children under five; the servants and slaves. Warm water come bubbling up out of the ground; endlessly it seems! They say it is healing, and well it might be, it felt so relaxing to bathe in!

Then we were served a delicious meal. They say that Bursa is a town that even Alexander the Great spent time in. He liked the way they fixed meat so much that the meal we ate is called Alexander's Kebab, after him. There are heaps of delicious, fresh pide bread placed on each platter. This is topped with meat which has been cooked on a spit, slow roasted, and sliced off as soon as it is cooked. These thin curling bits of meat are arranged on the bread, and topped with a tomato sauce and a slice of thick yogurt. Over it all they pour boiling butter. It is simply delicious!

They say winter gets cold here, because we are in the foothills of what they call the Big Mountain, or Uludağ. I think it perhaps seems cold because they are comparing it to other locations near at hand which are warmer. But my guess is that it's about like home. We'll see. It won't be a problem in the harem, as we have great fireplaces and personal braziers, which are kept well stocked.

Thank you for writing about Aunt Jelena. It is no small thing for her to write out Epistles. She is an amazingly dedicated woman of God. Please give her and dear Aunt Olivera my love! Handwriting takes such lengths of time! Even the few chapters I copied out to bring with me took so long, as you remember. But I'm glad I have them and those Scriptures I committed to memory. These are my greatest treasures.

Please give everyone my love. I shall miss you especially this Advent and Christmas season, as these are not celebrated here. A big kiss to little Vuk from his Auntie, who hopes one day to be able to meet him!

With all my love,
Mara

Mara did love to write and so she put her hand to learning the Turkish calligraphy. It was fun choosing a character and decorating it with letters. She made one for each of the children in the palace. Şehezade meant "princess".

She was a shy girl, with curly hair and a dimple in one cheek. She leaned on Mara's shoulder and beamed the whole time Mara drew her picture. Mara chose a crown for her, with flowers, and it came out beautifully.

Erhundu was a serious little girl with big, dark eyes. Mara wanted to make her smile. Her name was difficult to draw out, seeing as it meant something like "meritorious deed well done". After some thought she drew hands holding a tray with a cup on it. She shaped the tray and cup into the letters of Erhundu's name. The child stood at her elbow the entire time, entranced. For the final bit she took the little girl's hand in hers and had her dip the chiseled feather in the ink and make the strokes with her. Her face lit up and she smiled. Mara showed her how to blow gently on the page until it was fully dry. Then she gave her a little kiss on the cheek and handed her the finished piece. Smiling she took it to her mother, full of awe that she had been chosen to receive such a treasure.

Mehmed was a bouncy boy, almost four. His name meant "praiseworthy." Since he was apt to take the picture and fold it into any number of shapes, she made him a paper bird from the beginning. This way he could run and throw it. On each wing she drew a calligraphy of his name, in mirror image. She made sure the paper she chose was sturdy. He ran with it to his mother, laughing with delight. Then he ran back to Mara and gave her a hug to thank her.

Fatma was a chubby baby, the little sister to Mehmed. Because she was too little to appreciate calligraphy, Mara drew her a little picture book instead. She sewed the pages together and used it to help her learn words like apple, cat, bird, cup, tree, sun, and stars.

When he was home from war or commissioning great works in his empire, Sultan Murad occasionally strolled through the harem, checking things out. It so happened he was there the day when Mehmed discovered that he could take his folded paper bird and set it to flight from the upper balcony. It landed on his father's turban. The sultan thought he had been hit by an actual bird and set to swatting about his head. When the combination of shouts from his son, and slave girls running to his rescue produced the paper bird, slightly bent from its collision, he laughed. Mara was immensely relieved. For a few moments she imagined loosing her head for the creation of this dangerous fowl. But the bird was returned to Mehmed, who was consoled when his father patted him on his head and called him brave. Emine Hâtûn explained that Mara was entertaining the children with paper and calligraphy. He approved and asked to see some of her work. It was Fatma's book of pictures which ended up pleasing him the most.

Snow in Bursa was deep and crested in drifts that required special teams to shovel paths so market and social life could proceed. At least this is what the women in the Harem were told. Inside the warmth of the Seraglio, life was cocooned and warm, except for the moments one left one's room to cross the courtyard and gather in one of the common rooms. Then there was a blast of cold air and wet slushy snow to contend with. But it lasted only long enough to make the warmth inside feel more inviting.

Mara loved the cold. It reminded her of home, so she tried to find an excuse to be the person sweeping the courtyard each day. Hands tucked in mittens her mother had knit for her years earlier, she would sweep a path in the freshly fallen snow each morning. Sometimes the little children would want to be outside with her, but the mothers rarely let them.

There was a universal fear that cold might make them ill. So Mara mostly enjoyed the time she had to herself with the brisk wind and bright snowflakes. An occasional bird found its way into the courtyard and cocked its head at her. She was sweeping one morning when the announcement came that there would be guests within the hour.

The hibernation of winter left many of the women languid. Others were restive and eager for something to happen. Guests would break the monotony. A bustling and tittering of ladies awakened throughout the Harem like bees in spring. Soon most of them were gathered in the common room, children in tow. Extra touches were being added to the meal.

"The Vizier's wife, Aytan Hâtûn will be here," Hüma smiled, as Mara helped her keep Mehmed from getting distracted as they hurried down the corridor, "she is a known storyteller and poet. She is the one who explained to me that my name Hüma means the Bird of Paradise."

The men would, of course, be meeting in the Selamlik. It must be a Divan gathering of the counsel that was bringing the men for a long enough visit that they were bringing their wives.

Mara brushed snow off of Mehmed's clothing. He had run off to taste snow and landed face down. He didn't mind, and was no worse for wear, so she used the edge of her kirtle and he was ready to run into the room after his mother.

There was a bustle of *Gözde* and servants, *Ikbal* and and *Kadın*. The children mostly clung to their mother's skirts, although a few, like Mehmed, were bold enough to venture near the trays of food which beckoned tantalizingly near the window. Emine Hâtûn came in, leading the guest. Several of them were new to Hüma, but were eventually introduced.

Aytan Hâtûn, the Vizier's first wife, was clearly the eloquent and cheery leader. She stood taller than the others around her, an ermine-lined crimson robe flowing from her shoulders. At her elbow was a certain Mahtab Hâtûn, who was one of the wives of Hızır Pasha, the governor of Amasya. Although more diminutive in stature, there was something about the intensity of her visage that heightened Mara's sense that she should be alert. A third lady turned and Mara recognized the wife of Saruca, the Beylerbey of Rumeli. He it was who had escorted her to the wedding in Edirne, and had helped arrange the details with her father. He was a kindly old man and his wife Asal Hâtûn had been kind and helpful. Even now, seeing Mara, she pulled away from the group and came over to give her the customary cheek to cheek kisses.

She held Mara at arms length and admired the wardrobe, "The air here is doing you good, child," she said, "you look well."

"Thank you, Asal Hâtûn," Mara bowed, "I am doing very well, it is kind of you to notice."

"And this one?" Asal Hâtûn asked, tousling Mehmed's hair.

"This is Hüma Hâtûn's son," Mara smiled, introducing the two ladies to each other, "he is one of my favorites here. And with his mama so busy, I occasionally get to play a bit."

"I'm glad to see you so happy, my dear," Asal Hâtûn approved. "I would …" she started to say when Mahtab Hâtûn appeared at her elbow.

"And who do we have here?" she crooned, placing a long, crooked finger

227

under Mehmed's chin to lift his face to hers. Her burning gaze scared the child and he hid his face in Mara's skirts.

"Sultan's sons should not hide their faces," she said disapprovingly, "you must train your son better!" she turned to Mara, shaking the long finger in her face. "And what a strange amulet!" she reached up and pulled the key necklace out from under the scarf Mara wore at her neck. No one had even seen she wore it before. Several of the women stopped to pay attention.

"It's a key," said one, "why isn't it in your key bag, on your *cevberi*?"

"Ohhh!" one girl drew her breath in sharply, "that's gold! Where did you get that?"

"Someone's currying favors," insinuated a sharp nosed girl with a suspicious air.

"Ladies, ladies," Asal Hâtûn interjected, "we are blocking the door to the room. Please."

Mara didn't know what to say. She didn't have the time to. Mahtab Hâtûn had swept on to the next group of women. By the time Mara caught her breath, Asal Hâtûn was gone too. She quietly tucked her necklace back in place, but felt dirty somehow.

The ladies all settled on the pillows. Servants filled the low tables with food, making sure to use the interior doors so that no winds from outside would disturb the women.

Emine Hâtûn made announcements and introductions, and then said, "It is my hope that our dear Aytan Hâtûn will regale us with poetry and spin tales as only she can."

She turned and nodded to Aytan Hâtûn adding, "Thank you for gracing us with your presence, here in the depth of winter. You have brightened our days by going out of your way to show us this favor."

Aytan Hâtûn smiled, responding, "The kindness is yours, Mehd-i-ulya. It is an honor to be here, and we know that going out of your way to host us only adds to your burdens. This kindness is benevolent and one we can not hope to equal."

The servants kept passing new dishes. Lamb slow cooked in quince and pomegranates was followed with eggplants stuffed with cracked wheat and chickpeas in pepper sauce. A deep dish of rice in minted yogurt sauce was paired with pickled stinging nettle in lamb and lemon. Jerusalem artichoke in olive oil with carrots came next, with fresh bread and hummus. Mara kept busy feeding Mehmed. She wondered where he tucked the food!

Abdiya Wesab

The sun broke in brief intervals from behind the clouds, sending momentary brightness in their midst, followed then, once again, with fresh flurries. After the *Gözde* were asked to dance, Emine Hâtûn again asked Aytan Hâtûn to honor them with a story. Hüma settled Fatma on her knees, and began rocking her. Mara made Mehmet a toy doll, shaping her cloth napkin. She wasn't sure he would sit still much longer. Out of the corner of her eye she noticed Mahtab Hâtûn watching them, and again felt uncomfortable.

Aytan Hâtûn leaned back and closed her eyes, smiling. She began to rock gently back and forth after the nature of *meddah* storytellers. Softly, in a sing-song voice she began to entertain them.

"Once there was, once there wasn't, when the donkey was mayor, and the camel was the town-crier, and I was rocking my grandfather in his cradle." She began, "The revered teacher and hodja known to all his people as Nasreddin the Beloved was tired. He had walked to market, because his donkey had a lame leg. The sun was hot and beating down on him. To his left and right fields of watermelons spread, the heat shimmering on their wilting leaves. Sweat collected along the edges of the Hodja's considerable turban."

Mehmed surprised Mara by sitting still and listening. She smiled. Perhaps stories would be how to regale a boy of his age. She looked over at Hüma and caught her attention. They both giggled at the depth of his concentration.

"Nasreddin Hodja finally saw a tree in the distance," Aytan Hâtûn went on, "reaching it he lay down to rest, tucking his turban under his head as a pillow. Gazing up among the branches he perceived that the tree held walnuts. Hanging in tiny orbs the little walnuts cheerfully danced in the breeze.

"Nasreddin, being the great imam that he was, allowed his body the rest it needed, but his mind was busy as usual. Gazing up at the strong tree and the tiny fruit he pondered. 'Allah is veritably God the Magnificent and most Excellent,' he said to himself, "but I wonder if it was efficient for him to give such a strong tree such tiny fruit. Look at these wide and strong limbs. They could easily hold a field worth of fruit like those poor watermelons I passed in the fields. Then those fruits would not face a dearth of nourishment in the blazing sun.

"Being weary, Nasreddin drifted off to sleep, but was rudely awakened when a walnut fell from the tree and hit him on the head. Jumping up and rubbing his head he cried, "Allah be praised! If this world had been designed upon my poor advise I would have been just been killed by a watermelon. Allah be praised!! He is surely wise!" And Nasreddin Hodja never again questioned the wisdom of Allah."

The women clapped politely as the story came to an end. Mara glanced down at Mehmed. He had fallen asleep, lulled by the story. Hüma pulled the edge of her kirtle up over him.

"That was delightful Aytan Hâtûn," Emine Hâtûn decreed, "Its been too long since I've heard that wise tale. Well done!"

With some coaxing Asal Hâtûn was cajoled to give the history of Osman. She too was an excellent *meddah*, and Mara found herself learning how Osman's father Ertuğul was Bey of the Kayı tribe. Entering in service to the Seljuks of Rum he was rewarded with the Lordship of the town of Soğüt, a frontier with the Byzantine Empire.

Osman, his son, became Bey when his father died. Faithfully he served the Seljuks with battle raids against the Byzantines. Taking land he gained Bapheus, Phrygia, Bithynia, and with it notoriety among the Seljuks who began to honor him for the dexterity with which he wielded the Sword of Islam. Osman was also a disciple of a local dervish, a Sheikh Edebali. One night when he was sleeping at the dervish's home he had a dream, which he then told the dervish upon awaking[36].

Asal Hâtûn began to croon a song to explain the dream,

"From your holy chest arose
A sickle moon that gently glows.
From your heart it grew, and then

Abdiya Wesab

Into mine did powerfully bend.
To my surprise it was a seed,
Symbolic of our holy creed.
From my navel it did spring,
Branched about began to swing;
A tree it was, strong to behold
Its leaves were made of perfect gold.
It grew until its shade was wide
And all the world could fit inside.
Encompassing the world around,
Within me was this mystery found.
Behold the mountains and the streams
Were flowing from me in my dreams.
A fountain that could serve the world
A banner from my heart was furled.
The people to me flocked to drink,
This puzzles me and makes me think."

Mara listened to the haunting tune and
the gifted voice of the singer. The

women around the room were swaying to the music, joining in, for many of them knew this song. As it ended Asal Hâtûn returned to the story, quoting the dervish,

"'Osman, my son,' he said, 'Allah has revealed to you that you have been given the imperial office and your descendants. In celebration it would honor me for my daughter Malhun to become your wife[37].'

"And thus we have the honorable family that hosts us today. Osman was the father of Orhan, Orhan the father of Murad I, Murad the father of Beyazid I, Beyazid the father of Mehmed I, Mehmed the honorable husband of father of Mehd-i-ulya, and father of our most excellent Sultan Murad II, Allah be praised."

"Thank you, thank you, Asal Hâtûn!" Emine Hâtûn said, clapping for this performance, "Truly the Ottoman Empire is springing up from Osman, as you so powerfully told us, and we are delighted to sit in the shade of its branches!"

The servants were serving coffee to each woman, in the traditional small porcelain cups that were called *finjans*. Mara was not yet accustomed to this intensely sweet beverage, if so it might be called. It was so thick that it might be likened to a soup, but perhaps should have been called an elixir, for the dose was so small. She had heard that it was used to strengthen awakened thoughts, but hadn't noticed any significant impact on herself.

Mahtab Hâtûn was talking, and Mara turned to listen. "Now ladies," she crooned, "I must show you the latest benefit of these small *finjan*. Styled as they are, perfect for coffee, they are also created for discerning one's fortunes!"

A murmur went up among the women. To know one's fortunes? How curious! Mara's spirit however instantly knew that this was part of why the Lord had made her sense that this woman wasn't all that she appeared to be.

'You must be blameless before the LORD your God,' Mara remembered from Deuteronomy 18, 'Though other nations listen to conjurers and diviners, the LORD your God has not permitted you to do so.'

"As soon as you reach the dregs of the coffee, stop drinking," Mahtab Hâtûn was saying, "then turn your *finjan* over and bring it to me. I will read your fortunes for you!"

She made it sound so exciting that many of the women hurried to finish up their drinks. Mara began quietly praying.

"Oh, look here!" Mahtab Hâtûn looked at how the grounds had run down the sides of the cup for one of the *Gözde*, "you have a most delightful fortune pending, darling! Soon you will catch the eye of the one you love and bear a son worthy of being Sultan!" She chucked the girl under the chin as if she were a child and reached for another woman's *finjan*. Then stopping, she looked over at Mara.

"You, there, with the scared little boy, come here," she ordered. All eyes turned to Mara. What could a Fortune Teller want to single one person out. It must surely be either very exciting or extremely disastrous!

Mara shook her head gently, "Thank you so much for the offer Mahtab Hâtûn, but the child is sleeping on my kirtle and I would not like to disturb him."

"See now how she spoils that child!" Mahtab Hâtûn's voice got shrill. The room was galvanized. Even Mehd-i-ulya, whose kingdom this was, seemed curious.

"I beg your forgiveness, Mahtab Hâtûn," Mara said softly, "but the child's not mine, I am merely helping to care for him."

"You can go if you wish," Hüma interjected, feeling guilty that somehow her son was causing problems she wasn't aware of.

"See, even the mother of the child gives you permission to come," Mahtab Hâtûn said triumphantly, "bring your *finjan* to me. I am curious about your Fortune."

"Thank you for singling me out, Mahtab Hâtûn," Mara said, feeling her heart rising to her throat as she spoke, "but I would not like my fortune read."

"Oh, getting all haughty with us now, are you?" Mahtab Hâtûn sneered, "listen to her, girls, are we not good enough for you? Who are you anyway to insult a guest of the good Mehd-i-ulya in this fashion?"

Mara hung her head and chose to be quiet. She prayed under her breath, hoping that she would not have to say more.

Abdiya Wesab

After a moments silence Mahtab Hâtûn raised her voice more, "This one, who is she that defies your hospitality, O house of the Sultan?"

Mara felt a tear slip down her nose. She had never been so publicly humiliated before. But she knew that she would hold her ground if she had to. Emine Hâtûn spoke up,

"She's new, Mahtab Hâtûn," she said gently, "and I'm sure she doesn't mean an insult. You are thoughtful to offer to give Fortunes. Let Fortune smile on those who are eager to receive it. If she is reticent, so be it. It is only to her own loss."

Mara breathed a sigh of relief. And Mahtab Hâtûn acquiesced to Mehd-i-ulya's wishes. Mara puzzled how it was that this woman had even seen her necklace. It hadn't even be exposed.

Mara's relief, however, was short lived. Before the guests left that day Mahtab Hâtûn came over to Mara and said quietly in her hearing, "I know who you are, and see you are unfaithful to the House of Islam. Beware!! The Sultan does not bear a Sword in vain!"

As spring crested, Murad took the *Kadın* and *Gözde* on a trip with him. As Sultan he had now more than quadrupled the Ottoman Empire. Considering that the attack of Timur had almost eliminated them, this was some progress. As the carriage drove through the countryside, he talked about the the three seas which were now at least partially theirs. The Aegean had but a few troublesome islands left to conquer. The Mediterranean, although only beginning to have an Ottoman presence, would expand. And the Euxine Sea with its colored history was almost half theirs.

So it was natural that their destination was the coast. Because it would take all day to get there, it was decided that the entourage would stay several days. Such a packing up and getting ready it was! Mara marveled when several oxen carts full of food and servants went ahead of them by a day to set up camp. The littlest children would be coming along. So she offered to help Hüma with Fatma so that she could get her family ready. Jiggling the baby on her knee she hummed little tunes and Fatma laughed when she made funny faces.

Hüma stopped and looked at her part way through the packing. "You're different," she said, "there's no reason why you should bother yourself with my children, but you're always available and the children feel safe with you. I can tell. A mother knows."

Mara smiled. "Thank you, Hüma, I feel honored. I've always loved children."

Hüma smiled watching Fatma. She was a sweet little girl. Her brother was more than a little impetuous to make up for it! But when his energies were channeled in the right direction he could use the intensity to be creative.

The trip was delightful. Once again Mara drank in the beauty of creation. Just being outside, even in a carriage, was something she treasured beyond description. Thankfully it had rained two days earlier, so there was no dust clouds on the roads. The Sultan's entourage was protected in front and behind by mounted guard, and all whom they passed stopped and dismounted, kneeling in homage, as was the custom. Once they left the city and were out in the open there were far less people, and the horses got off to a steady clip. They drove past fields where people were working in the distance, and through forests with quiet shade. Several times they stopped and took a break. At one lookout they picnicked. The Marmara Sea shimmered in the distance, inviting and almost incandescent on the horizon. Mara picked several bouquets of wildflowers.

As they went on Mara wove garlands of vetch, chamomile and wild roses, offering them to the other *Kadın*. Before long the terrain changed. Olive trees clambered down steep hills to the water, interspersed with vineyards. Bright murmurings of starlings danced in unity across the expanse of sky. Ringed plovers chattered on the edges of fields, giving their hallmark, plaintive warning cries, pretending to have broken wings to distract hunters from their young. Shepherds with meandering flocks moved ewes with their young across the emerald fields. Everyone was in high spirits. They would soon arrive. No doubt the water was cold. Even so, just to see so much vastness and beauty, and have this adventure was a delight.

When they arrived the servants had their quarters ready. The water was right there! They went down and put their toes in. Yes, it really was cold! But the pleasure of that gentle lapping of tiny waves, and the colorful sky tinged with sunset was refreshing. Mara lingered after the others went in watching the sky for the first stars. There was something about the end of a day that was satisfying. It was a sign of God's consistency; His Presence; and the Promise that He held all things together by His Word which had spoken this all into being.

The little *Gözde* who had had her Fortune told, who was predicted to be singled out and noticed by the Sultan had gained his attentions and was along on the trip. When she saw Mara alone she sidled up to her.

"Did you notice that I've been chosen by the Sultan?" she pointed out, looking demurely at her hands, but with an expression not unlike a cat about to pounce on a mouse written all over her face.

"Oh I'm so pleased for you," Mara smiled, "what is your name, dear?"

"Ayna," she said.

"That means 'mirror' doesn't it?" Mara asked.

"Indeed it does," Ayna nodded.

"It doesn't surprise me that the Sultan noticed you, you are very beautiful."

"Thank you," said Ayna primly, "but you see it was because my Fortune was read that I was chosen."

"Interesting," Mara responded carefully.

"And if you had done your Fortune, you could have had a good future too, but now, who knows?"

"I am happy for you that your wish has come true, Ayna," Mara smiled at her, "and I'm happy to get to know your name. Where are you from?"

"I'm Türkmeni," Ayna answered, "but I'm talking with you about this because you chose ill-fortune for yourself by not honoring Mehd-i-ulya that day. Just wait and see, it will come back to haunt you!"

And with that she walked away, not at all interested in having a conversation, but only in casting blame. Mara was puzzled that she should go out of her way to take this upon herself, when even Mehd-i-ulya hadn't taken offense at the event, but she struggled it off. Perhaps the girl was just jealous

Abdiya Wesab

Supper was a festive affair, with music and a bonfire. Poetry and minstrel tales wove themselves together with the sparks and spun upward.

The Sultan was in fine fettle. He picked up a *saz* and serenaded the women of his Harem. The long handle of the *saz* cast shadows away from the fire, like a finger pointing across the water behind him. He strummed the four stringed instrument and sang,

> Hark! The nightingale's lay so joyous:
> "Now have come the days of spring!"
> Merry shows and crowds
> On every mead
> They spread, a maze of spring;
> There the almond tree its silvery
> Blossoms scatters,

Mara Hâtûn

Sprays of spring:

Gaily live!

For soon will vanish, biding not,

The days of spring!

Tents for pleasure

Have the blossoms raised

In every rosy lane;

List' to me, if thou desirest,

These beholding, joy to glean:

Rose and tulip, like to maiden's cheeks,

All bounteous show

Whilst the dew drops,

Like jewels in their ears,

Resplendent glow;

Do not think, thyself beguiling,

Things will aye continue so:

Gaily live!

For soon will vanish, biding not,

The days of spring[38]!

Mara listened only in part. She was enthralled with the fresh air, smell of smoke and water, and the simple delight of being outside.

In the morning Mara was the first one up. The water was like glass. Since they were on the Asian shore of the Marmara, the sunrise would be panoramic. Wrapped in a shawl against the predawn chill, she went down to the waters edge and had the grandeur to herself to drink in.

"Thank You, Father God, Creator, that You have Graced us with such beauty. It feeds my soul. Thank You. Thank You Jesus for living in me with such Mercy; show my heart ways to reflect Your Glory today. Thank You Holy Spirit for breathing in and through me, for praying through me, for giving me the mind of Christ." She paraphrased Romans 5:17 to herself, "Death once held me in its grip, and by the sin of Adam and Eve, death reigned as king over all people. But now, because of what You did, Jesus, I am held in a much more powerful grip: Your grace! You empower me to reign as royalty in this earthly life. Not because I am born into royalty, or married into it, but because of Your blood Alone. I get to enjoy True regal freedom through the gift of perfect righteousness you give me in Your covenant Jesus. Thank you!!"

As she was coming back to her tent she saw Ayna near the opening. She whispered a good morning, and smiled, but Ayna looked flustered and hurried past. Mara felt badly that she couldn't seem to befriend this girl.

That day she wrote to her parents, and painted them a small picture of the sea. She had grown fond of calligraphy and miniature painting. There were so many vantages to paint from here, out in the open!

In the afternoon, as they sat around, having tea, Sultan Murad gazed westward. "Over there," he pointed, "the fleet is now strong enough to blockade any place I send them. Venetian ports in the Adriatic and Aegean have given us a tentative peace. Their commerce is important to the Empire. When ships come and go, and roads are safe, there is good economy. Over there," he waved to his right, "Europe is seeing the benefit of being united under the Sultan. With wars settled and done, the Balkans at least are replanting their fields and building strong towns."

Mara hadn't internalized that Europe was the shore she was seeing across the water. Waves of memories flooded her mind. That was home, over there. Her aunt Jelena managed a monastery just around the corner. Her parents were just a little north west. Vuk was growing up without his auntie just across that water.

For a moment she swallowed hard, but the Holy Spirit within her gave her comfort as she silently took her emotions and placed them at the foot of the Cross. Jesus had died to empower her to walk out living and reigning in life, no matter what the circumstances. She was not controlled by her emotions, she had the power to choose.

"I choose to live in the here and the now." she told herself, "like the birds of the air, Father God is watching over me where I am, and caring for my loved ones even while we are separated from one another. Bless them Lord; let them feel Your Presence today."

Murad was still talking. "I've developed a wonderful solution to help control the new territories of the Empire," he was telling them. "It's called the *devşirme* system. As you know all Ottoman lands belong to me, as Allah's representative on earth. I lease it to the *Spahis* or military leaders, who provide troops to serve us in proportion to the amount of land held. The peasants who live on the land, work it to provide income for the *Spahis*. Now we are strengthening that with the *devşirme* system. One in five boys born to families who are not Muslim will be tithed to me. They will come into my service to be trained in the military. They will come as children, become Muslims, and be raised up to be the front line men. Those who prove themselves and conquer new lands for the Empire can become local rulers. This new branch will be organized into an infantry. I have called it the *Yeniçeri* or New Force. Isn't that brilliant?"

A murmur of support rippled through the *Kadın*, *Gözde*, and servants. Of course anything the Sultan said must be met with approval. There was no second opinion considered. He was Allah's representation on earth. He knew best. Mara kept her thoughts to herself, but inside her heart was crying. One in five little boys from her own towns and villages to be taken from their mothers as children, and forced to become Muslims?

"Father God, have mercy upon us," she prayed. She sensed Holy Spirit whisper He had placed her here, right now, so she could pray, and He pray through her. That gave her both zeal and peace, knowing she could simply breathe and lift this to God and He would intervene as He knew best to do.

For a minute she felt she was lifted to heaven and got a bird's eye view of the situation. The Sultan had swooped in, and conquered most of the Balkans. As a result, any who were living there had a choice to make. If they chose to accept Islam, they were absorbed into the Muslim population. This could give them status in their own community which they did not formerly have. They would not retain their minority name, but were now Muslim.

Under the Ottomans this meant that any "infidel" who became Muslim was now a Turk. Their benefits included the menfolk joining the conquering hordes and coming away with war booty. Men could now marry several wives, build a harem, and keep concubines as well.

They could work their way up the social ladder quite successfully.

This also meant that those who chose to retain their Christian or Jewish faith were moved to minority status. Mara suddenly understood this testing was something that God could use for good. Now they were called 'infidel' or *'gavur'*. Under the Ottoman Empire they were a recognized religious minority. As such, Christians and Jews could never be seen as anything but inferior. This testing of their faith would help people choose what they really believed.

But Mara also keenly remembered why she had put her own life on the line. Many had fled ahead of the wars, taking their skills and expertise elsewhere, outside the Empire, leaving all they had ever known and valued. Her family had hosted many refugees fleeing northwest. Destruction and fire, looting and raping was part and parcel of this Islamic take over. Most conquered cities had lost their libraries, places of worship, cultural landmarks, and centers of learning. Many of their leaders were killed or forced to flee. It was a diminished and subdued people who now faced these choices. Many were war widows and orphans. Already as vassals they were paying a heavy tax. Now they would also have their sons taken. Her heart was heavy. But she felt Jesus pulling her to look up to the sky and listen.

Mara looked up and saw the vastness of the sky, studded with luminous clouds and reminded herself that she was seated in the heavenlies with Christ[39]. "Thank You God," she smiled, looking up at the depth of the sky overhead, "You know to go before all that happens, even when I don't know what to ask. You give into my heart the prayers that need praying. You say to ask for Your kingdom on earth as it is in Heaven, and then you place me where I need to be to know what I need to ask. So I can rest in the Promise that You have a Victory planned, in spite of this. Bring Your Good; I know You will." She reached up to finger the necklace and realized it wasn't there.

For a second she felt faint, then she reasoned that perhaps she had forgotten to put it on when she got up in the morning. She had gone out to look at the water early. Maybe it was still under her Bible beside her bed?

As soon as she could she slipped back to her tent and looked, but search though she might, it was no where to be found. She retraced her steps with no luck. Finally she went hesitantly to Emine Hâtûn.

"Mehd-i-ulya Hâtûn, please may I ask a question?" She initiated, bowing down. This was brave. She had always only ever responded to Mehd-i-ulya Hâtûn. She was unsure as to if it was even permissible. The great lady nodded, granting permission.

"It is a small thing, Mehd-i-ulya Hâtûn," Mara said quietly, "but the necklace my aunt gave me is gone."

Emine Hâtûn looked up sharply, "are you accusing someone of stealing it?"

"I ... I don't know, Mehd-i-ulya Hâtûn," Mara said, "I left it beside my bed this morning when I went down to the water to watch the dawn come. With all the bustle of a new day I forgot to put it on and only just remembered when we were listening to the Sultan. When I went back to my tent it wasn't there."

"I see," Emine Hâtûn said, looking Mara in the eye, examining her to see if she told the truth. She was satisfied.

There really was no reason for Mara to lie, "I will look into this."

"Thank you so much, Mehd-i-ulya Hâtûn," Mara bowed, " I am sorry to be of trouble."

Mehd-i-ulya Hâtûn announced the loss at the next meal, challenging everyone to look around outside, insinuating that perhaps a link of the chain had broken, and someone might find it. It was a wise approach. This way who ever took it might redeem themselves. But no one came forward, and, in the end, Mara went home to Bursa without it. She grieved its loss deeply, feeling that she had betrayed her Aunt's trust by being careless. As she watched the undulating hills roll past, she prayed quietly in her heart, asking the Lord to find and return her key to her.

Sultan Murad II took advantage of the death of Hungarian king Sigismund in 1437 to re-enter Serbia and check the fidelity of his subjects there. Mara did not initially know that he had gone.

The *Kadın* were taking advantage of the sunlight and embroidering the fringes of gowns that were going to be used at the upcoming wedding of Halime Hâtûn's son Prince Alaeddin. Halime herself was in Amasya with him, getting everything ready. Yeni Hâtûn was teaching a new set of *Gözde* how to do their hair with jewels. So it was just Emine Hâtûn, Mara and Hüma.

Mara Hâtûn

Emine Hâtûn spoke up suddenly and said, "you had best be appealing to Allah for the success of the Sultan on his current raid. I received word today that he is in Serbia. King Sigismund died and he is making sure that the balance of power remains in our favor."

Mara looked up quickly. She felt the blood rush to her head and was almost dizzy.

"Yes, you," Mehd-i-ulya looked severe, "you're the one I am talking to. Allah must help the Sultan succeed and find obedience in his subjects in your realm. There's rumor of trouble."

"I am sorry to hear this," Mara said in a subdued voice. She was genuinely

273

sorry. So much hung in the balance, for herself, her people … "I will be praying," she looked Emine Hâtûn in the eyes, "thank you for informing me."

Her genuine sorrow and surprise satisfied Emine Hâtûn and she changed subjects. The list of wedding guests was long. Prince Alaeddin and his older brother Ahmet both had a list of in-laws who would be coming.

"Halime Hâtûn must be besides herself with joy," said Hüma.

"Yes, events like this are well suited to her personality," Emine agreed, "at her wedding, it was a fanfare of enormity. She is the Sultan's first wife. To celebrate, he gave his sisters away as brides to

Halime's brothers. Because Halime's people were former enemies, they were granted the chance to show their loyalty in generosity. Because it knit two Muslim tribes together, the celebrations went on well past a week! Such a wedding it was!"

"Ahmet and Alaeddin have proved themselves and come of age," Hüma agreed, "they rule in the footsteps of their father."

"Yes," Emine Hâtûn nodded. "Gone are the days, I trust, when brothers fight each other for the Sultan's throne. I am proud of my son. He has grown this empire so significantly that there is plenty of territory for second and third sons to rule portions of it."

Abdiya Wesab

Mara was only partially listening. She knew King Sigismund's family well. He and her father were allies, and had been so for far longer than Halime Hâtûn's family had been aligned with the Sultan. Her heart grieved that war kept happening, and men conquered and force people to be subjects.

More immediate questions were bubbling in her heart. Grgur had moved north to Hungary with little Vuk and his good wife. Were they safe? Her brothers were vassals to the Sultan, but had former agreements with Hungary. How did that stand? How hard to be caught in the tension of a faith that united them with Hungary, and a forced peace with the Sultan brokered by her marriage.

Mara Hâtûn

It took all her self-control to remain outwardly at peace and avoid poking her finger and ruining the wedding garments she was embroidering.

As if reading her mind, Emine Hâtûn glanced over, "the war in Europe will soon be over. We needn't worry ourselves about it. The Sultan is doing so well with his trusted men. Each one who proves himself is being set to rule domains he has conquered. It's a fair and square deal. But you know that already. The girls that are being trained in the harem will become the prize award brides to those in power. Under them the *devşirme* is growing, and revenues flourishing. My son is a wise man. He is creating a system that proves to any natural and sensible man that becoming a Muslim is profitable and just, and the only way to advance in today's world."

It was well that the wedding was an elaborate and festive occasion, festooned with memories that everyone could return to. Great tables were laden with Halime Hâtûn's family traditional roasts. New traditions were shaped by modern inventions that layered the spun sugars of Bursa between the finest and thinest layers of dough the kitchen could provide. The *Gözde* danced with candles in their hands, which caught the light of their jewel bedecked hair. Ayna made sure that she came and pointed out to Mara that she was not part of the dance routine because she was a pregnant woman now. Mara told her how happy she was for her and offered to help her. Ayna turned up her nose at this,

"I will be sure to only accept help from women who are true to the faith and loyal to the Sultan!" She snubbed, and again walked away from Mara.

It was well that memories of a happy wedding cushioned the Sultan's household for the coming blow. It was only weeks later that galloping horseman delivered the news to the palace in Bursa: Prince Ahmed had died and his house was in mourning. Because Allah had so willed, and *kismet* had brought this sorry loss of the Sultan's oldest son and heir, Alaeddin was quickly placed in his brother's stead and took on the mantle of heir. Halime Hâtûn had lost a son, but had not lost her role as the future Mehd-i-ulya Hanım. She grieved as a mother, but not as one who had also lost all hope.

Back at the harem, each mother held her children a little closer, realizing the tentative nature of life afresh. Once again Mara quietly gave thanks that she was not required to provide offspring and devoted herself to the children around her. Once again Ayna found a way to sidle up to Mara.

"Fortunate for you to not have a child that can be killed like this, Mara Hâtûn, am I right?" she said snidely, shocking Mara. Had she read her mind? Ayna was not finished, "one has to wonder if women like you don't curse the household."

Again she walked away, head in the air. Mara felt an arrow pierce her heart. How cruel for Ayna to talk like this! Mara went to the Lord about it that evening, in the quiet of her room. She went over to her little couch and knelt beside it. Turning to the Word of God she whispered Psalm 57,

"My soul is among lions, I do lie down among them that are aflame; Even the sons of men, whose teeth are spears and arrows, And their tongue a sharp sword. Be Thou exalted, O God, above the heavens; Thy glory be above all the earth. They have prepared a net for my steps, My soul is bowed down[40].*"*

Tears ran down Mara's face. It was true. Ayna's words had pierced her heart like a sharp sword. She felt the Lord whisper, 'Ephesians six.'

Turning there she read the chapter and realized that verse sixteen addressed her issue, "… take up the shield of faith with which you will be able to quench all the flaming arrows of the evil one."

Instantly she felt encouraged, "Yes, Lord," she whispered. "Ayna doesn't mean to, perhaps, but her words are sharp and the evil one is trying to use them as flaming arrows. I truly felt them pierce my heart." She picked up and hugged the Bible, "yes, Lord, my faith is in You, Lord of heaven and earth, you alone are God. With your Word, I quench these flaming arrows right now, and I thank you Jesus for your blood which washes me. Without You, Lord, I could not proceed. Thank you!"

As she placed the Bible next to her bed and turned to get up she felt a shadow pass her window. Glancing around she saw no one there. Shrugging she pushed the feeling away and went to bed.

The next morning Emine Hâtûn came to her. "You speak several languages, Mara, yes?" she asked.

"Latin and Greek, Mehd-i-ulya Hanım," Mara answered, "and Serbian."

"Good," Emine Hâtûn responded, "you are to start teaching Mehmed Latin and Greek. It is only a matter of time before he will be sent to a tutor. He needs a head start."

Mara was relieved. With Ayna's verbal attack, she had assumed that Emine Hâtûn would have something negative to say as well. She took note in her heart that Ayna's issues seemed to be personal, and she wondered why.

Mara was only too glad to spend more time with Mehmed. It was summer, and a delightful time to take ones inks and parchment outside. She taught him the various scripts and their sounds, letting him use her calligraphy pen. She also included Latin and Greek in the circle games and songs she sang with the rest of the children, knowing that Mehmed would learn best if it were fun.

Mara played clapping and hoping games, and taught the children how to count, to rhyme, skip rope and learn poetry. While she taught all the children who were present, her focus was Mehmed. The other children came and went, but he was captivated. When Mara asked him why, he turned his big eyes on her and solemnly said that now that he was the biggest boy at home he needed to get ready to be a good ruler.

Sometimes the other mothers sat and watched. It intrigued them that Mara could keep their children occupied for great lengths of time. While this was the wing for *Kadın*, occasionally Gözde wandered into the area, especially if one of the *Kadın* was teaching them something.

Occasionally Mara would look up and find Ayna standing there, watching her. At first it made her heart jump, remembering all the negative things she had said, then she decided to pray for her when she saw her, hoping it would soften her heart. One late summer day she looked up and Ayna was sitting with the *Kadın*, great with child. Mara realized her time was coming soon. As the children were happy playing alone, she came over and sat down.

"It's nice to see you again, Ayna," she smiled, "how are you feeling?"

Mara Hâtûn

Ayna tensed up and looked sideways at the other women, "why'd you be asking? Do you want to put curses on me too?"

"What could you possibly mean, Ayna?" Mara was dumbfounded, "I don't curse. I never have, I never will. And I've only ever been friendly to you. You puzzle me."

"But Ayna says you have a book of magic in your room that you use at night," Halime Hâtûn said solemnly.

Mara's tongue cleaved to the roof of her mouth in shock. Witchcraft was a serious accusation. She gathered herself and breathed a prayer for help. "Halime Hâtûn," she ventured, "would you be so kind as to come and search my room? I'd like to know which of my books has magic in it so we might burn it right away."

Mara's response surprised the women. After a second Halime rose to her feet and came with Mara. "Please come along," Mara invited the others, "perhaps one of you will spot something I am failing to see."

Ayna was taken aback by Mara's open trust and slunk along behind the *Kadın*, not sure where this was going to go.

Mara invited them all in, and opened her chest, taking everything out and laying it on her bed. Each book she had, she opened and handed to Halime

Hâtûn, doing so respectfully, answering every question they had.

She explained to them that each language used a different way to write. Ottoman Turkish used the Arabic script, the font in her Bible was in Cyrillic script, the manuscript where she practiced Latin was in Latin letters and the her parchment with Greek Scriptures was in the block letters common to their texts.

Ayna peered around the others, examining and fearful, almost, of coming in the room. When she saw the Bible, she pointed, "That's the one she uses!" she said triumphantly.

Mara breathed another prayer. Burning her Bible would not be acceptable. Picking it up she realized that she could read from it to them.

"In the second chapter of the Quran there are many references to the book of Psalms, which is in this book," she explained, "The Quran quotes a Psalm, in Surah 34:1, "Praise be to God, to Whom everything in the heavens and everything in the earth belongs, and praise be to Him in the Hereafter,"" Mara quoted.

Then she opened her Bible to Psalm 115, "Listen," she said, translating as she went, "May the LORD give you increase, both you and your children. May you be blessed by the Lord, the Maker of heaven and earth. The highest heavens belong to the LORD!"

She looked at them, "You see, this is like the Quran. It is my Bible, in my own mother tongue. I read this every night to pray to, thank, and bless God."

She lifted up the Latin and Greek manuscripts. "These are written in two other languages, the ones that I am teaching the children because Emine Hâtûn asked me to. I believe she wants Mehmed to learn a few extra languages so that he is better able to interact with people from other countries."

Hüma was standing in the group, "Read once from the Greek, Mara," she said, curious.

Mara turned to Psalm 89, "The heavens are Yours, and also the earth. The earth and its fullness You founded. North and South You created ..." she read, then looked up smiling, "There are more than one hundred Psalms to praise God with. I love them all."

Halime shrugged her shoulders, "I don't see any witchcraft here," she began, turning to Ayna, but the *Gözde* had slipped out and left the group.

The *Kadın* looked at each other, then Hüma said, "I'm sorry, Mara, I'm not sure why she is so suspicious of you, but thank you for being so honest. I hope it cleared her thoughts."

"Thank you all also for taking the time to listen to me," Mara responded, "we are women from many different countries gathered here. Perhaps Ayna is just lonely for her own people and wanted some attention. I pray that we can be good friends to her."

That evening, once she was alone, Mara closed her curtains before falling to her knees and praising God for His protection.

The extremes of first wedding, then funeral left Mara grateful for the simple peace of being able to peel cucumbers and shell peas by the fountain. Halime had left to be with her son again. A more settled camaraderie had grown between the rest of the wives.

Mara wasn't quite sure why. She sensed a jealousy, but wasn't sure who was jealous of whom. It did seem that Yeni Hâtûn was more peaceful with Halime gone.

Shelling peas, she hummed quietly, listening to the fountain and the contended tinkle of tiny peas bouncing in the bowl as she shelled them. Yeni Hâtûn came over quietly to join her and Mara was finally able to ask her what her real name was.

She looked surprised that anyone would want to know. "It's Ertine," she replied simply, "no one else ever asked."

"That's such a pretty name! What does it mean?" Mara went on, glad to see a response from Yeni Hâtûn.

Ertine looked up quickly, then back down at her hands. "It means jewel, or something precious in the language of my people's ancestors," she said.

Mara smiled, "I thought so! That suits you completely!!"

Ertine looked shocked. "I wouldn't have thought so," she responded.

"Why not?" Mara asked gently.

Ertine stopped and looked out across the courtyard. She was silent for some time. Mara almost thought that she hadn't heard the question. Then she responded.

"My mother died young, and my family did not like girls," she said simply. "I was a bother to them, and got in the way. The only time I was of value was when my father could exchange me for a bride price to arrange a political alliance with the Sultan."

Mara had stopped shelling peas to listen. This was the longest she had ever heard Yeni Hâtûn speak.

"That would make me very sad if it were me," Mara sympathized.

Ertine looked at Mara, "You are different, somehow."

"Because?"

"You listen and ask questions. I mean, you seem to want to know me."

"Of course! We are sisters here. You are a nice person and I'd like to get to know you."

"I ... I've never thought of that," Ertine puzzled. "I mean, I guess because Mother died young, and I was alone until the Sultan came, I never really had anyone to talk to."

"That's sad, Ertine!" Mara said, "I'm really sorry. I wish I had asked sooner, but I've only recently learned enough of the language to be able to talk clearly."

"It would be nice to be, what did you call it, friends?"

"It would," Mara smiled, "and I don't want to ask you anything you don't want to talk about. You can ask me questions too."

"Really?"

"Of course!"

"So why are you so different, then?"

Mara was quiet for a moment, listening to Holy Spirit. She sensed that she could be honest.

"When I was a child my parents explained to us that all of us, boys and girls alike, are created by God our Creator and He loves us equally."

"That couldn't be!" Ertine was shocked, "my nursemaid told me that girls are damned and only boys are of value to Allah. In fact she told me that the Prophet Muhammed, peace be upon him, was shown a vision of hell, and it was populated with women[41]!"

"Perhaps that's because Allah and God are different?" Mara ventured.

"Really?" Ertine leaned forward.

"Yes. God our Creator is the One who made us. In fact He loves us so much that He Himself came down to earth and became a human called Jesus. He chose to be a man so that people could relate to Him, but also to pay the price for sin. As we know, the punishment for sin is death. So He chose to let Himself be killed, but then, because He is God, He overcame death and rose from the dead, taking the keys of death away from satan. When I learned that, I saw how great His love is. Some might die for a good person, but God chose to lay down his life as a sacrifice for all of us."

"That is different than Allah, I see," said Ertine slowly, "and it makes sense. God makes something, He loves it, and He rescues it. Allah is different. He is a judge, and we must work hard to stack up good deeds so that when we die we might have enough good done to get Him to let us into paradise."

"You are right, Ertine," Mara nodded, "and so I chose to follow the God who loves me. And when I did, He gave me a gift."

"What's that?" Ertine asked.

"It's called the Holy Spirit. God describes Himself as Three-In-One, as Trinity. Just like you are a daughter, a wife and a mother, yet you are Ertine. God is our Good Father, and also our Redeemer Jesus: the One who died and rose from the dead, and also Holy Spirit. The Holy Spirit comes and lives in our hearts if we choose to follow God. That's what makes me different, Ertine. It's not me, it's the Holy Spirit living in me."

"How do you follow that God?" Ertine asked.

"You simply thank Jesus for coming and dying to pay the price for your sins. You talk with Him in your heart. That is called prayer. Then you ask Him to forgive your sins and move into your heart. He will walk with you and show you what's next."

Ertine was quiet for a moment. "I'd like that," she said simply. She closed her eyes and lifted her hands, like they all did at the beginning and end of meals. "Good Father God, thank you for sending Jesus to die for my sins. I want to be like Mara, and be happy. Can you forgive my sins and send Holy Spirit into my heart and make me different please?"

Mara smiled as she watched Ertine's face change. In a minute she opened her eyes in surprise, clutching at her chest. "It's true!" she whispered, "I can feel light in my heart! It's … it's like someone is in there, sweeping."

Mara prayed for Ertine quietly, agreeing with her. Gentle tears started rolling down her cheeks. "He said that He loves me," Ertine whispered. Her eyes flew open. "God loves me?"

Mara nodded, smiling.

"It feels like I have butterflies inside me!" Ertine giggled.

Mara laughed and clapped her hands! "Yes, Ertine! God's happiness feels that way sometimes! I'm so happy for you!"

"Will you teach me more, Mara?" Ertine asked.

"Of course!" Mara smiled, "But God Himself will also teach you a lot too. If you ever have a question, just ask Him."

She was going to say more when she noticed that several *Gözde* were coming around the corner to the patio. She and Ertine waved and invited them to join them, but then they saw the expression on their faces. Something was wrong.

Mara Hâtûn

"What is it, Sisters?" Ertine asked them. Both she and Mara got up to see what they could do.

"We can't find Emine Hâtûn, and Ayna's time to have the child has come early," one of the started.

"She's having difficulty, blood came with the water," a second one inserted.

"Can you help us find Emine Hâtûn?" a third interjected.

"Do either of you know anything about birthing?" the first finished her sentence.

Abdiya Wesab

Ertine and Mara looked at each other. "Mara, I'll go to Ayna," Ertine said, "Can you find Emine Hâtûn?"

"Of course, dear!" Mara said and began hurrying from room to room. She alerted the servants to help her, and within minutes found Mehd-i-ulya discussing meal plans with the steward. As soon as she heard the news she sent a servant to get the midwife. She ordered another to gather the birthing materials, and told a third to put on a pot of hot water and see that it was brought to the *Gözde's* quarters.

Mara and Mehd-i-ulya Hâtûn hurried together along the corridors to find Ayna. When they reached her side, it was evident that she was delirious with pain.

She was not clear where she was, or who she was talking with. Ertine was bathing her forehead with a moist cloth and cooing to her, several of the girls were hovering around, worried and uncertain. One was rubbing her feet with oils, trying to be helpful.

"Help me!" Ayna screamed, groaning as she went into a contraction, then coming back out she screamed "mother, come and see, the Fortune, the Fortune, my son will be the Sultan!"

Mehd-i-ulya Hâtûn, Ertine and Mara looked at each other. Then Emine Hâtûn clapped her hands. "Girls, Ayna needs some help," she said calmly, "I have been at many births. She will do fine. It will help her most if you will all calmly do what I say."

She looked around the room. "Suna, clear a space over there for the kettle of hot water that the servants are bringing," she nodded to one girl, who instantly obeyed. "Fatima, build up the fire and keep in going, without any smoke. Do not leave it unattended for any reason, do you understand?"

The girl called Fatima nodded and set to work. Emine Hâtûn turned to the one rubbing Ayna's feet, "Do you have the birthing oils there, Asuman?"

"Yes, Mehd-i-ulya Hâtûn," she responded.

"Get lavender and start massaging her belly, then bring the scent and waft it under her nose. It may help slow the birth." Emine Hâtûn ordered. Asuman obeyed.

"Mara, quickly mix basil, rosemary, cardamom, peppermint, rosewood, bergamot, and rose. Rub these gently on her forehead, temples, wrists, and back of her neck. It should bring her to her senses."

Mara obeyed, praying that the Lord would come and relieve and revive Ayna, and that His Peace would fill the room.

As they were talking the midwife arrived. She and Emine Hâtûn assessed the situation. "The child is breach,

Mehd-i-ulya Hâtûn," the midwife stated shortly after conducting her inspections. "But its heart is beating fine, we simply need to help it turn around."

"I thought so," Mehd-i-ulya Hâtûn said, "please take over then, and command any of us to assist you as you see best."

Mara admired Mehd-i-ulya Hâtûn for stepping in and being able to first take charge, and then step back and give the authority to someone who was more skilled than herself.

Thank you, Mehd-i-ulya Hâtûn," the midwife bowed, "I am honored by your trust, I believe that we will all work together for the best possible results for this lady and her child."

"My son, my son!" Ayna screamed, correcting the midwife mid-contraction.

"My lady, you are laying down," the midwife went on, "which may be half your problem. You are going to do some movements with me that will be uncomfortable to you, but will help your baby come out. Is that agreeable to you?"

Ayna started crying, "I don't want the pain. Take the pain!"

"Ertine stroked her forehead, "Dearest, if we listen to the midwife, you will have less pain, I promise, I have given birth too."

Ayna looked at her with big eyes for a second, then closed her eyes again and nodded. "If we must, then I will, for my son," she whimpered.

"Good girl," the midwife approved, "so, we need to get on all fours, like this," and she dexterously got down on all fours to demonstrate, "but I need you to do so in the middle of the room, so that I can then feel which way the baby is. You are still early enough in your pregnancy that I hope to turn the child." She pointed to Ertine and Suna, "you two, help her up and bring her here."

Gradually, Ayna was able to get on all fours. When she stood up, however, there was a clink and jangle and something metal hit the floor. Ayna was crazed with pain and didn't even notice. The rest of the room suddenly froze. There, on the floor, was Mara's necklace.

Mehd-i-ulya Hâtûn grimaced and strode over to pick it up. Silently she passed it to Mara and nodded at her to put it on. The other women watched. It was honoring of Ayna that no one mentioned anything.

The midwife simply got down next to her and felt the child. Gently she started massaging the infant, coaxing it to turn. The room held its breath. The contractions had slowed. Mara quietly prayed her thanksgiving to the Lord for answered prayer, and then blessed Ayna, forgiving her. There must be a lot of buried pain for her to have acted like this.

"You with the oils," the midwife barked, "mix a batch of lemon, bergamot, rose, chamomile, lavender, geranium and rosewood. Dilute this with apricot kernel oil and rub her back gently. Keep adding more oil each time you massage her."

"You there," she nodded at Mara, "grab some soft cloths and dip them in the hot water, then set them as compresses on her back right after the oil is applied. Keep changing them out to keep it warm."

Each of them set to their tasks quietly and quickly.

"You," she nodded at Ertine, "take another warm cloth and bath her where she will deliver the infant. Be careful to not be too hot or too cold. Keep a clean, moist, warm cloth in position there, changing it out as needed. And get geranium from the oils. As soon as she is clean, massage her with geranium at the opening. It will prevent tearing." Ertine obeyed.

"Now, my dear," the midwife continued after a few minutes of continued massage, "I want you to breathe deeply. You are surrounded by kind friends, you are in a safe place. In a little I will ask you to change your crying into roaring. You see, when we become mothers we each discover our own roar. When you roar, you can push better. But not yet, do you understand?"

Mara could see that the midwife was galvanizing Ayna and preparing her. Ayna had been sobbing and using her strength for the pain. This direction helped her pull herself together.

"One more thing," the midwife went on, "I need you to change positions for a few minutes. Keep your knees firmly on the floor and your legs straight, as you have them now, but gently lower your head and fold your arms. Rest your head on your arms. This will help me massage the child better."

Ayna groaned as she moved, but she obeyed.

"Well done!" The midwife praised her. She continued to massage the baby, gently manipulating it to turn it around.

"You with the oils!" she said, "prepare a mixture of equal jasmine, sage, fennel, elemi, and lavender, in apricot kernel oil. Have it ready."

"You," she said to Suna, "listen carefully, I am going to give you a longer list of oils. Mix them in equal parts in apricot kernel oil, and stir it in a small bowl. Then braid Ayna's hair in two braids so you can reach the back of her neck and begin rubbing her shoulders and neck with these, are you ready?"

Suna went to the oils and nodded.

"Rose, palmarosa, bergamot, chamomile, jasmine, lemon, rosewood, spruce, hyssop, geranium, angelica, orange, frankincense, sandalwood and lavender... did you get that?" The midwife said, grunting a little, with her head also down under Ayna's body.

"Yes," Suna said and set to work. She was careful to not pull Ayna's hair as she worked. Mara continued to change out warm and soothing cloths on Ayna's back, quietly praying for her and the baby as she did so. She marveled how the midwife keep all these details in her head.

"Now," the midwife breathed, "I am going to push a little harder, and it may hurt, but then the baby will come out easily."

Ayna whimpered, but braced herself. Mara realized that having all these oils, and the loving presence of so many friends focused on serving her was probably the best support she could have received in this moment. She was feeling loved, and this quieted her. When the midwife had to push harder she cried out, but didn't panic as she had earlier.

"There!" the midwife leaned back on her knees. "There, you did it! The baby is turned around! Good for you!"

The midwife looked around the room. "Can someone fetch the birthing stool?"

"Of course," said Mehd-i-ulya and went.

"Thank you Mehd-i-ulya," the midwife bowed when she came back, "now Ayna, my dear, it is time for you to get up. First onto all fours, slowly, then you will come and sit on the stool. We will change the massage oils and help you give birth. Are you ready?"

Ayna nodded and slowly got up. Suna and Mara helped her to her feet. The midwife placed the stool under her and began giving out new orders. The mix that had been used on her back was now to be rubbed on her wrist and ankles.

The oils which had been prepared and set aside were rubbed on her lower back and abdomen. Gradually the contractions returned.

"Now, my dear," the midwife smiled, looking Ayna in the eye, "are you ready to roar?" She had positioned herself on the floor in front of the *Gözde*, and was calculating the regularity of contractions and the position the baby was in. Ayna nodded.

"Keep looking me in the eye, then, and each time you have a contraction, add your voice to the pain and roar. With the roar, push." the midwife directed. "And you who are rubbing, keep doing so, gently."

The baby came surprisingly quickly. The process from birth, delivering the placenta, cutting the umbilical cord, and oiling the baby was completed in under two hours.

What took a little longer was calming Ayna when she realized that the child she had birthed was a girl, and not the son her fortune had promised.

(D)ara only learned years later that simultaneously to the Sultan's reoccurring advances in Europe, the Pope was finally responding to pressure that Janos Hunyadi's had been requesting for years. Perhaps, if there had been a concerted effort earlier, this season of war and Mara not knowing her family's fate would not have gone on for years.

The Pope organized a new Crusade to join Hungary and Venice and counter the Ottoman presence in Europe. The Pope told the leaders that they were not bound to earlier peace treaties they had been forced to sign with Sultan Murad.

Now the Sultan met resistance and was not pleased. He was attacking Serbian provinces that he did not rule, Belgrade in particular. His men were ravaging Hungary, and he expected Mara's brothers to serve him. He was ready to replace any weak or unwilling vassal with direct Ottoman rule throughout his Empire. Using threats of more raids and conquest north of the Danube, he further weakened those on the edges of his boundaries in Europe.

Abdiya Wesab

The attack against the Sultan came from an unexpected source. One of his brother-in-laws, Karamanoğlu Ibrahim Bey of Anatolia began attacking in the east while the Sultan was in the west. Gathering his son Alaeddin and his army, the Sultan and his heir charged across Anatolia to stop this attack on the Ottoman Empire. Ibrahim repented and sued for peace, at which the Sultan returned to Bursa for a brief respite, while Alaeddin went home to Amasya.

No sooner did the Sultan get home then an urgent message came from Alaeddin's wife, Selvin Hâtûn. She had found her husband and both of her sons strangled! She was beside herself. The timing on this was strangely curious. Was Karamanoğlu somehow involved?

The Sultan had been called home to grieve his son Ahmed only a a few years earlier. His death was reported to be an accident, but now the Sultan wondered. The news of Alaeddin's murder grieved the Sultan deeply. It was no secret that this son had been his favorite. Murad was cut to the heart. The grief and shock in the Harem reflected his sorrow.

Mara felt that his grief was also full of anger, and it was justified. Imagine killing the Sultan's son and grandsons. How terrible! She could hardly wrap her mind around it. But when he was in the Harem he seemed angry specifically at her. She could not imagine why.

Emine Hâtûn soon confirmed what Mara sensed. Things were not going well in Europe and the Sultan sensed betrayal from her father's family. She felt trapped, unable to change anything, yet caught in this machine of war and the struggle for power.

Although a funeral was generally conducted when and where the person died, being the Sultan's lineage, the bodies were brought to Bursa to be buried. Halime and Selvin Hâtûn came with hollow-eyed grief. Only one small child, a little girl called Selvi had been left in the slaughter. The child clung to her mother's neck.

Gradually it was found that a Kara Hızır Pasha had crept into Alaeddin's quarters by night and performed this heinous act. Mara puzzled what manner of man could first of all move up in rank to be a Pasha, and then stoop so low to commit such a ghastly murder. Eventually she learned that this Pasha was Alaeddin's personal advisor[42]. How could one trust anyone then?

Perhaps this explained why the Sultan seemed so suspicious and angry. If what Emine Hâtûn said was true, and Mara's brothers were not being loyal to the Sultan, he could suspect her of being an accomplice. How would she ever prove her own personal loyalty, apart from being present and faithful?

Mara spent a long time on her knees by the arched windows that night. Her heart was turned to prayer, knowing that it was her only key. She fingered her key as she prayed. A full moon shone down into the courtyard, filtered only through the leaves of the lemon tree closest to her room. Mara prayed and felt God's Peace, reminding her that He was on the Throne. She could not solve this murder, or the grief. But she could love this grieving mother and wife. She would be there for the precious little girl, Selvi. She could not solve the war in Europe, she could only be faithful to her promises and pray, asking that God would bring about His Will.

Young Mehmed was nearly eight. What with him now suddenly being the next son in line to be Sultan, and this coming of age, his time for a personal tutor had arrived. The Sultan ordered that he be moved to the district of

Manisa and be trained to be a "tested son." He was to learn how to fight and govern. The bustle around the palace was subdued, overcast as it were, by the specter of Alaeddin's death. Mehmed's mother Hüma Hâtûn was pregnant again, and now that she was suddenly mother of the Sultan apparent, great care was taken to keep her resting. In fact, she had been ordered to full bedrest when she fainted early in the pregnancy.

Mara offered to help her pack up her son's items. Mehmed ran about gathering everything eagerly into a pile in the middle of his royal chamber. His hair was tousled, his cheeks flushed.

"I'm to be Sultan, Auntie Mara," he jumped up and down, "I'll have sword fights and great steads and tell everyone what to do!"

He plopped down on the window seat and gazed out across the courtyard, suddenly silent, lost in thought. The stormy clouds racing outside which only moments earlier had seemed to fuel his pace now tossed unseen beyond his unfocused gaze. Turning slowly he fixed his sight on Mara, who knelt by his piles of things, folding and stacking them.

"I knew it," he whispered, almost talking to himself, "something told me I would rule." His voice grew firmer. "I was born to be not only sultan, but also the see... What is that title? The ruler of the Rûm?"

Mara Hâtûn

Mara looked at the child who but yesterday had been the rambunctious boy who always got into trouble, running too fast, throwing things not meant to be airborne, eager yet tripping, wild, like a young, unbroken colt.

"Do you mean Caesar?" Mara smiled at him.

The darkening clouds behind him framed his pale and serious face. His shoulders went back and he stood proudly. As if to accentuate his statement a low rumble of late-winter thunder rolled around the valley and echoed off the mountain. It was the whisper of the very mountain once called Olympus, revered by rulers for centuries. With the thunder the clouds spat a smattering of hail against the window.

"Yes!" Mehmed said firmly, adding emphasis with a firm stomp of a slippered foot. "The Caesar of Rûm. That will be me."

"Well, Your Honor," Mara bowed her head slightly, both to hide her smile at his childish zeal and to show him the deference this show of power desired, "shall we ask for chests or baskets for this mountain you are packing?"

Mehmed came back into focus and evaluated the situation. Then he marched into the hall and ordered servants to bring him chests. Mara shook her head. Whatever this child did become, he was certainly getting a head start. Folding his silk kaftans she had a flashback to her own brothers in their youth. Royalty though they were, they had been charged with shoveling out the stables and following the horses at plough before they were trusted with swords. She hoped that Mehmed would learn to sweat under more humbling circumstances than giving orders, else he might be distanced from his subjects in ways that would weaken his rule.

Raised here in a house of women, surrounded by fountains, music and tasty morsels was a charmed life, but apart from her little attempts at teaching him language and letters, he had only stories to base his ambitions on. The watery winter light coming in the window was suddenly darkened. Glancing up her heart leapt. It was indeed March. If she were not charged with helping a budding king pack his wardrobe she would have risen to twirl and clap with the joy that welled up in her. A muster of white storks! These wise ones knew the fickle storms of spring were momentary. Bravely they were pushing north against the wind.

"Take my love with you," she whispered, fingering the key around her neck.

Yes, storks were the harbinger of spring in Bursa, blessing home and turret alike with their clicking murmurs, but back home in Serbia the advent of storks was a celebration. These very birds, perhaps, would soon be nestled in the tall nooks of her father's land. At home the village women would have tied colored wool in their hair on the first of March. At the first sighting of the brave muster they would run outside and throw the wool after the birds, laughing and clapping. Then gathering the fallen bits of wool, they tied them in the bushes to give smaller birds blessings for their nest building endeavors.

Mara sighed. She had no real news from home, if her home even remained standing, and how her family was. Reminding her heart to remain focused she picked up the last silk robe and found the crumpled and well-loved paper bird with her calligraphy underneath. Cocky and crooked, it brought back the memory of the Sultan dancing about, thinking he had been hit in the head. Smiling she smoothed the culprit out and set it on top of the pile of clothing she had folded.

With Hüma on bed rest, Mara went to gather a tea tray for her. She wrapped her shawl close about and stayed in the shelter of the overhang. The hail had spent itself and was reduced to graupel, riming the edges of what would shortly be fresh snow. A knot of sparrows chattered in the rafters, seemingly concerned about the shifting season. Mara breathed it in, deeply. She loved the sharp, keen crisp air with the promise of snow. Spring snow had a certain pungency that carried the hint of almond blossom and expectant soil.

Mara Hâtûn

Helping Hüma was a pleasure. They had become best friends by now, almost like sisters. Mehmed and Fatma were happiest when they could be with their mother and Mara. Most of the winter afternoons Mara had coached Mehmed in reading and writing. Fatma sat there and listened, enthralled with the way the pen moved across parchment.

Now that Hüma was bed-ridden, Mara helped her at the children's beditme, singing to the children, rocking Fatma gently, sitting at the feet of Hüma's bed, so that her children could be near her.

But now Mehmed was eight. Usually Hüma would have gone along to his appointment in Manisa, but since she was expecting the baby, she needed to stay in the Harem. It was decided the boy was to go with his newly appointed tutor, and Hüma would follow when her infant was old enough to travel.

Hüma bade Mehmed farewell with tears, kissing him again and again. He however, was excited about his future, and brushed it off. He was a man now, and needed no tears to thwart his onward goals. A sword and a good fight was what he wanted!

The family had been up before dawn to see Mehmed off. The journey was long and early travel was safer than being on the road late at night. Armed guards and a battalion surrounded this third son of the Sultan. Security was increased double, no triple, and worry hung in every shadow. The carriages creaked and groaned, wheels cracking the glazed ice in puddles that had thawed the day before. Sabers and swords rubbed in sheath and scabbard. The horses pawed and blew, cracking cold leather and adjusting themselves for the long haul. The *Kadın*, of course, remained behind lattice and the confines of the Harem, audible only to each other as they waved scented handkerchiefs.

Mara was glad that the edge of night was peeling off the eastern horizon as the entourage left. The moon hung low and sleepy on the western horizon, the sky swam with heavy stars. A few doves complained briefly in the eaves, wondering at the noise. This startled a fish owl, whose surprise woke the caged *bülbül* near the entry. They shook and tried their voices, but when the cover wasn't taken off their domicile, they settled back, head under wings, with only minor chagrin.

Mara hurried back to comfort Hüma, bringing her some fresh *sahlep* to drink and massaging her feet with oils. She knew it was hard on Hüma to not even be able to leave the bed and wave her son off with the rest of the women. As nice as rest was, Hüma felt the weight of her confinement. Sighing she leaned back against the pillows.

Mara stirred up the fire in the brazier. The wind had stilled with morning, leaving a dusting of snow to brighten the world and add a touch of adventure to this auspicious trip. But it also made the palace colder. Mara went to the cupboard where the feather comforters were kept and brought an armful to Hüma's quarters. Fatma had stirred, but not fully woken in the farewell.

Knowing she was too heavy for her mother to hold right now, Mara laid the sleepy Fatma on her own legs, straight out before her, with a pillow on her feet. Cuddling an added comforter around the child she rocked her back and forth with her knees. Quietly she sang her the little lullaby she had learned in Turkish,

"Fish, fish boatman fine,

In the evening we will dine.

It will be a *byrek* of mine,

Fish, fish boatman fine[43]."

Fatma dozed. Hüma was tempted to sniffle. Mara first told her about the heavy moon and bright stars that accompanied her son on his journey, then seeing that this did nothing to help, Mara asked her questions to brighten her thoughts.

"Tell me about your childhood, Hüma," she began, "I realize I don't even know where you are from."

Hüma smiled a little, almost chagrin. "It's true. You'll have to tell me about your home too then, Mara, promise?"

Mara nodded.

Hüma rolled over on one side to face Mara better. "If I tell you my real name, will you keep it a secret," she whispered suddenly. "It feels like my name belongs to my story, and I haven't told anyone else. I … I'm supposed to be Hüma, named by Emine Hâtûn, as is appropriate. And I like Hüma, for it means "bird of Paradise." I do love birds so."

Mara smiled and nodded, "I love birds too, Hüma. And I'd be honored to know your real name. I'll keep it to myself. It's nice to have two names!"

Hüma began in a whisper, "My real name is Stella. It means star. I like to think that my son is riding to Manisa by starlight! My family was from Salonika. Father was a Rabbi. He was respected in our community and led the congregation like a shepherd. My brother Timon left for France well in advance of the war, and found he could not return. It is well he didn't come. The war would have forced him to fight, capitulate to Islam, or die."

She was silent for a moment, remembering. Mara was also lost in thought, thinking of her own brothers. Such a strange world where the only hope of doing something to retain the family land, or freedom to keep one's own country, culture, religion and traditions was … was gone. Gone unless something bigger happened, like a uniting of European countries, or another order for a Crusade. But even those had proven useless. The Ottomans were too powerful, too well organized, too well funded, and ... she stopped herself. This wan't about her, this was about Hüma, and she wanted to listen well.

"I understand, Stella," she murmured guarding the depth of her feelings from escaping with her voice, "may I use your name?"

"Yes, please, but only when we are alone. I don't want to infringe on the order of things."

Mara nodded.

"Well, Timon was gone, and Father fell sick. Otherwise we would have also gone to France I think. I heard my parent's discussing it. But it didn't work out that way."

Stella rolled over onto her back again. "Would you mind putting a pillow under my knees, Mara, if you can reach one without waking Fatma?"

Mara reached and passed her a pillow. That was easy, the room was made of pillows almost. "So what did you do then?"

"Well, Father died and Mother and I were left to survive on our own. Before things got bad we used to go up into the hills to a place where she lit candles. I was forbidden to talk about it. But as I got older I learned it was a church. Since Father was a Rabbi I was confused. But it turns out that Mother had come from a Christian family and married into the Synagogue. A little unusual, but it worked for them."

Mara looked at her friend. "So did your parents introduce you to God?"

"Not really. I mean, we went to synagogue, and Mother secretly lit candles at church, but neither set-ups helped us. The Ottomans came in the end. Mother and I were carted off to the slave market and separated. What I wouldn't give to have her here to help me with this birth."

A tear rolled down Stella's cheek. "Mother used to sing me a little song when I was a child. It made no sense to me, but I loved the tune. I've hummed it to my children many times, but seeing Mehmed leave this morning, I understand."

"I'm so sorry, Stella!" Mara said, "That's heart rending. I can't even imagine not knowing where my mother is. Could you, would you mind, sharing your song with me?"

Stella sang, in her clear voice, but the words, of course, were in her mother tongue. Mara closed her eyes and listened. Although the haunting tune was unique, Mara heard in it the whispers of wind-torn branches of pine trees protecting nests of migrating birds. She felt the tang of rosemary by the ocean. Behind her eyes she saw the rolling fields of home, green, but separated from her by a chasm. She opened her eyes abruptly. Stella was leaned back into her pillow, silent.

"That was incredible, Stella!" Mara whispered, "what did those words mean? I could feel them in my heart!"

Stella thought a moment and then whispered,
"Journey through this life
In search of one another
Always feeling compelled to search.
We keep on fooling
Ourselves into love.
Into life, hoping, wishing for this.
Hoping, wishing for this.
An endlessness, we just about give up
Until she comes in our memory.

Abdiya Wesab

A beautiful heart, a warm smile,
A fleeting glance and all is better.
A beautiful heart.
A warm smile, fleeting glance
And all is better.
You find for yourself
That things change you[44]."

"That's beautiful, Stella," Mara said, "When you sang it, I saw my homeland, but also islands in the sea that I've never been to. As you explain the words, I understand why."

Stella nodded, "Mother sang a lot. I wish she was here."

"I'm so sorry …," Mara began, but Stella was lost in her memories.

"Once I hit the slave block, it was only moments before a huge black eunuch came and chose me. It's all a confusion in my mind. I ended up here, and was given the name *Hüma binti Abdullah.* Of course, *binti Abdullah* means someone who has become a Muslim[45]. They never even asked me. That was what I had to be. Gracious! All these religions! Jewish, Christian, Muslim! What difference does it make, anyhow? None of their gods have solved my problems."

Mara held her peace, listening, "I'm sorry you went through that, Stella," she added quietly.

"I used to go up on our roof that overlooked the sea. I had doves. They were like friends to me. In summer we slept on the roof, under the glorious stars. In winter I could just go up far enough to feed my birds, and feel the wind off the sea. I miss that."

"I should be thankful. Here I am, a chosen wife of the ruler of the Ottoman Empire. Today we entrusted my son to his tutor, and he is the heir apparent of this throne. This was not what I expected in life, but it seems *kismet* has suddenly turned and the goddess of fortune shed light on my weary path. But I don't feel any pleasure in it. I wonder why."

Mara looked over at Stella. The tears had dried in streaks on her face. Her eyes were closed. This pregnancy was draining her of strength, but that was not the core issue.

"May I venture a guess, Stella?" she asked softly.

Stella opened her eyes, "sure, why not?"

"As you know I am a Follower of Jesus. I believe that those stars you slept under on the roof, and the birds you loved, the sea which you viewed sunsets over, and the baby you have in your womb are all made by a loving God, our Creator. He is not a distant God, commanding a legion of lesser gods to crush some people and shine with fortune on others. Nor does he delight in sacrifices, or religion, or rituals. So I see

God's interaction with people differently. He desires to be in relationship with us. I would look at your story and say that God loves you, and has a special call on your life. He has set you apart, and is working everything together for good for you because of His love for you."

Stella rolled over on her side and looked at Mara. The sky had brightened slightly outside the window. It cast a glow tinged with pink and orange against the far wall. "That is hard to comprehend. Besides, why favor me? I've never done anything to earn me God's favor."

Mara smiled. Fatma had flung a sleepy arm outside the blanket. Mara placed it gently back into the warmth of feathers and down, tucking the coverlet around her chin. "None of us can do that, Stella. I know people try. That is why there are so many traditions in every religion. But God is not in favor of any religion. If you read the Bible or the Torah you will see that God speaks very clearly against it. What God wants is for us to be His children, his beloved, his own. That is why Jesus came to earth. He is God incarnate; come in the flesh, so that he could pay the debt for sin that we each owe. When we accept that we can't earn our way to God, but that Jesus paid the debt we owe, Jesus cleanses us, and makes the way for us to relate to God as Father."

The light coming in the window was fully morning now, and the birds outside had chosen the chorus they were singing. Varied and purposeful each greeted day as if it were the first, in welcome awe.

"That's different, Mara," Stella said slowly, "when we observed the Sabbath, growing up, or when I went with Mother to light candles at her church, I felt like God was there, but just out of reach. It felt safe and good, but I left all that behind with the war, and becoming a Muslim. Now that you speak of God like that, I feel memories of that warmth and I miss it."

Her mug of *sahlep* emptied, she set it aside and pulled the blanket around her shoulders. Mara reached stirred the brazier with the fire iron.

"God is not far away, as some imagine[46]," Mara said quietly, "He is near. He is here now, actually. As a child, your parents did the best they knew to honor him. They sound like wonderful people. They introduced you to Him. Religion means many different things to various people. It's important you choose for yourself what you believe about God."

The tentative lilt of a garden warbler began in the orchard, beyond the harem wall. It was barely perceptible through the closed window and thick walls, but repeated as it was by others of its kind, the volume increased. Spring was clearly coming.

Abdiya Wesab

They fell silent together, Mara remaining prayerful. The morning shuffle of servants bringing breakfast to the rooms told them day had begun in earnest. In the hall the fountain tinkled quietly; the ever present background noise in the courtyard. Fatma stirred and woke, startling, but then smiled as she saw her mother and her "Auntie" Mara.

Ertine had quietly changed into someone who carried Light into the room. She smiled more, but this change was slower in coming, simply because the whole household was still in grief over the loss of Alaeddin.

The Sultan had to rush back to Europe and his war, but this time he took Halime Hâtûn with him, as far as the palace in Edirne. To distract himself, perhaps, he began to speak of renovations and plans for expansion of this northernmost palace. His mother, Emine Hâtûn and several new *Gözde* went as well. Eunuchs were left in charge of the palace in Bursa.

Before they left Emine Hâtûn gathered the three remaining *Kadın* and gave them a list of things they were to do for the deceased. A cloth was to be embroidered for Alaeddin's grave and Selmin Hâtûn would choose the pattern.

Ertine, Hüma and Mara were also to mind the children and oversee the stocking of the pantry for the upcoming Ramadan. Alaeddin's widow Selmin

Hâtûn, and her little daughter Selvi had been added to the household.

Until recently Ertine had been an unhappy mother. Mara now learned that a primary problem was that she felt cursed for having daughters. Erhundu and Şezade were wonderful little girls, and Mara always included them in all she did. Now Ertine began to value them as well. As their mother learned to smile, they did too.

When the four months and ten days of Selmin's mourning were over and they put away their black robes, Ertine was almost joyful. She and Mara had taken the little girls to play by the fountains while Hüma napped. Selmin Hâtûn came with little Selvi and Mara began doing a few circle games with the children, as she had often done in the past. This was new to little Selvi, having not been with other children much. She stood in the mottled shade of the lemon tree with her fingers in her mouth and watched, starry-eyed. Selmin smiled weakly, still drained from grief. Leaving Selvi she wandered off aimlessly. Mara noticed and drew Selvi into the game so Selmin could have some time to herself. Mara prayed for her, knowing that the shock of this senseless murder, and the dashing of every hope she might have ever had were still wrapped up in her widow *iddah*, or mourning period.

"Fatma, Erhundu, Şezade and Selvi," she said to the children, "look at that, you are a circle of friends, like the fingers on my hand."

She counted off her four fingers, naming each of them again. "It's good you take care of each other and are friends forever, yes?" she asked them, nodding to show that she was encouraging them to choose this. The little girls nodded and smiled back when she smiled at them.

"You are a good teacher, Mara," Ertine noted, "Ii you were a man you might become a teacher for a Sultan, you know so much!"

Mara laughed, "I didn't have to be a man to teach the future Sultan," she raised an eyebrow. Ertine laughed at herself, realizing that Mehmed had been Mara's pupil. Mara stopped and reveled in the moment. She had never heard Ertine laugh before.

"Ertine! You have a beautiful laugh! It's so good to get to know you better!"

Ertine smiled, "I think it's because Jesus is living in me now. I don't know that I knew I had a laugh before now."

The little girls pulled on Mara's hands, asking for more games. She smiled and taught them how to clap twice in front and once in back of themselves. It was harder than it looked, but they worked at it valiantly. Little Selvi bit her tongue to one side of her mouth while she reached carefully behind to get her hands to meet. When they did she was so excited she jumped up and down gleefully. They all laughed.

"I would just as soon teach the girls," Mara went on, "they are the ones who will raise future leaders."

"I learn so much just listening to you, Mara," Ertine sighed, "when I was a child, girls were condemned for being female."

"I hope that's changing, my friend," Mara said simply.

They joined hands with the little girls and did a small dance around the fountain in their bare feet. Two stomps to the left, two to the right, clap hands and bow ever so slightly. The little ones loved it.

"Soon you will dance like the true princesses that you are!" Ertine praised them. Just then they heard a shuffle and turned to see who was coming. It was Ayna. She was carrying her baby and looked sad.

"Come, dear, join us," Ertine sang out. "Look the little girls will dance to welcome their new sister!" Mara agreed.

Ayna flopped on the bench, dejected, almost not holding the baby, disinterested. Mara noticed that the child was thin and looked pale. Ayna had circles under her eyes.

"Are you not well, my sister?" she asked.

"How can I be well?" Ayna said petulantly, "the child is a girl, another unwanted female, worthy only to be thrown away. Besides, the Fortune Teller promised me a son who would be Sultan!" She nearly pushed the child off her lap in her frustrations.

"May I hold her?" Ertine wisely asked.

Ayna nodded indifferently. Ertine gently picked the baby up.

"She's beautiful," Ertine lied, "what name did you give her."

"Ogulgerek," Ayna said in a monotone.

Ertine glanced over at the young mother. She knew what the name meant and thought it was going a little too far. "Having a daughter whose name means 'you needed to be a son' reminds me of a story from my childhood, Ayna, may I tell you of it?"

Ayna shrugged her shoulders indifferently.

"When I was small my mother birthed a son. I had been first, but it took until he was born for my mother to get a name. I was given a new frock but when I was gleeful, my nurse told me the celebration was about my brother, not me," Ertine began. Mara noticed that Ayna was beginning to show signs of interest. "My nursemaid told me girls are a curse, and boys are a blessing. She said that when a girl is born spiders spin webs and the sun hides itself, but when a boy is born the midwife is paid well and everyone can finally rejoice."

Ayna nodded, "same in my land," she whispered, "I don't know what I did wrong to birth a useless girl. And why did the Fortune Teller lie to me?"

Ertine leaned over and patted her arm, "I know dear," she said, "look over there." She pointed to the circle of dancing princesses who were giggling by the fountain and had figured out how to add new steps to the dances they were creating.

Ertine smiled, looking at them, "two of those are my daughters," she said, turning to look at Ayna, "and I hated myself and my life for many years for failing to bear a son. I understand."

She watched Ayna's gaze go to the little girls playing together. Then she looked down at the child in her lap. "Ayna, I hated myself until Mara explained something to me."

Ayna looked quickly from Ertine to Mara and back. Her defenses were instantly intact again. Ertine spoke quietly, "Mara said that God the Creator made us female and male. He chooses who were are meant to be, and He loves us how He made us."

Ayna looked sharply at Mara then back at Ertine, "why would you believe her? She is a foreigner and doesn't know anything."

"A few weeks ago, when we went to her room, she knew the Quran and the Bible," Ertine reminded her.

"But why didn't you respect Mehd-i-ulya and have your fortune told?" Ayna hissed, turning on Mara.

"My experience with fortune telling is that there is no truth in it," Mara answered quietly, "I was not trying to be disrespectful."

Mara Ḫâtûn

Ayna slumped on her bench, "I see," she whispered, "just as happened to me. She said I would have a son to be Sultan. Did she say that to humor me?"

"I don't know, dear," Mara went on cautiously, "I can't get inside her head."

"But now I have a girl!" Ayna wailed, beginning to cry again, as she evidently did often, from the looks of her face. The baby heard her mother and began to whimper as well. Ertine got up to jiggle her.

"Ayna," Ertine spoke up, "when I was a little girl, if someone had loved me, I would have had a happy childhood. Instead I was cursed because I was female. Did you have the same lot in life?"

Ayna nodded, tears streaming down her face. Ertine turned to Mara. "Mara, what does your good book say about being female?"

Mara thought a second, "From the beginning of creation God made them male and female. Male and female He created them, and He blessed them. There is neither slave nor free, nor is there male and female, for you are all one. God blessed them and said to them, "Be fruitful and multiply, and fill the earth and subdue it[47]."

"Really?" Ayna breathed, "this is what God said?" For the first time Mara sensed that the real Ayna was coming out.

"Yes," Mara replied, praying quietly.

"It sounds to me like somehow we have been misguided," Ertine said. "A few weeks ago I made some choices I am glad of. One of the things I decided to do is give my daughters a happy childhood and not believe lies anymore. It became clear to me that I didn't choose to be a girl, and that God is the one who made me how I am. I am now happy being me, and I want my girls that way too."

"I see," Ayna said slowly, but in a way that made Mara see that she was actually thinking.

"I think," Ayna began, "I think it seems like the Fortune Teller might have lied to please me. I think … I think, Ertine that you have made a wise choice. I really wanted a son, and now I have a girl like myself. I think…. I… I see that I can either be upset and be miserable, or choose to change my thinking. I'm not sure I know how."

"I know what you mean," Ertine smiled, "it might take time. But we can talk whenever you want."

"Really?" Ayna looked at her quickly, checking. She clearly wasn't used to being valued.

"Yes, my dear," Ertine nodded, "I know what it's like. I have two daughters!"

"You're right," Ayna looked at the little girls, and then back at Ertine, "will you help me then?"

"Of course," Ertine smiled, "can I make a suggestion?"

"Yes?" Ayla asked.

"You still have a little time until the naming day. Maybe choose a name for your daughter that you would have liked for yourself?"

"Oh," Ayla said, suddenly thoughtful, "Nyazik. I always wished I had been called Nyazik. I always wanted to be graceful and able to dance, but that was not what our family did."

"What a pretty name!" Ertine clapped her hands.

"You are graceful, and a beautiful dancer, Ayna!" Mara said. "how special for your daughter to be named for the wonderful qualities you have!"

"I am?" Ayna said, genuinely surprised.

"You are," Ertine agreed, "and your princess will join her sisters here dancing gracefully in no time at all. But is she eating well? She feels light as a feather."

"She hasn't been eating," Ayna said, "and she cries a lot. You've had daughters. What do I do?"

Ertine thought a moment, then went into details about how to nurse on both sides, with the suggestion to feed frequently, to boost milk supply. She outlined how to make sure the baby is peaceful, not tense, and to be sure that she is latching on and not getting air. Ayna listened carefully. She fed Nyazik right away, and with a few adjustments she latched on and began to drink eagerly.

"Look at that," Ertine said, "you've got it! Both of you, well done!"

"Mara Hâtûn," Ayna turned to her suddenly, addressing Mara as a real person for the first time since that fateful day with the Fortune Teller, "why …why didn't you get angry at me for taking your necklace?"

Evidently someone had helped her piece together the details of what happened in the Birthing Room. Mara smiled at Ayna, "we all do things we wish we hadn't later. If I kept grudges it would make me miserable. Thank you for reaching out and joining us now. We would like to be your friends."

A weight dropped off of Ayna, and with it, a curtain was pulled aside that let her begin to associate with the other mothers and learn from them. Nyazik soon reflected her mother's change and was smiling within a few weeks.

In June Mara received a delayed letter from her parents. It was well worn, as if long enroute. Although it had a seal, it looked tampered with, and knowing the state of the war, Mara was not surprised.

She kept the letter in her bodice until afternoon siesta so as to have the delight of a read, all on her own. The heat rose softly from the clay tiles in the courtyard and crept into the front of her room, but the couch was cool and restful. Buzz of bees in the lemon blossoms and whisper of doves in the eaves gave the day's interlude a calmness that belied the way things were at home. It was a contrast

Mara struggled with. She fingered her necklace as she read.

Her parents didn't mention the turmoil. In fact their choice of words was very careful. She knew to read between the lines.

Dear Mara,

You will have perhaps heard that your brother's wife and little son have moved much further north, up into Hungary to keep little Vuk safe. Grgur has been captured and we are not sure where he is. Thank God, our health has been stable, even though there are many challenges. Stefan and Lazar try to stay in touch, but are not often home.

We have not recently heard how your sister is, but the last she wrote they are well, for which we praise God. Right now there is not much travel or transportation, and therefore little communication. We trust that you will get this small letter and know we love you. Thank you also for remembering us all with your love,

Papa and Mama

Mara looked out her arched windows into the nearly stifling tranquility. Not for the first time she felt that perhaps her sacrifice to be here had been wasted and pointless. Like a caged bird in a pretty prison, she was helpless to do anything, powerless beyond comprehension, and forced to keep silence when her heart longed to be active, alive, pertinent and useful. At least as a child she had helped her mother roll bandages and make food for the refugees. Here she was subdued into languid embroidery. Frustrated she paced her small room.

Murad had been gone for months now. Was her brokering of peace annulled? Did it even matter that she … Mara stopped herself and went down on her knees by the couch.

'I'm sorry, Lord," she whispered, "I must bring this to your Throne again. You know where my brothers are, and what is happening to them. Even evil and wickedness can be turned around to be used for our good and your Glory. Please, Lord, intervene. This season of war is ghastly. You see the plight of my family. My grief spills over."

Tears soaked the coverlet she knelt beside. The cooing of the mourning doves seemed heavy with melancholy, echoing her grief. "Lord, let Your will be done, and Your kingdom come in this situation. Please comfort and protect my family, Lord, and, if I may ask, let my sacrifice have purpose. Let me see that you are using this for your Good."

Instantly the Lord showed her Ertine and Stella. He showed her Selmin, walking away from their circle of friendship, locked in her trauma. He showed her Mehmed, Fatma, Erhundu, Şezade and Selvi. She felt Holy Spirit touch her heart with a peace beyond her capacity. Yes, the situation was impossibly difficult, but God had given her new sisters and five children to love.

He had a purpose in her being here. She got up from her knees refreshed and encouraged.

Summer waned peacefully in Bursa. Stella birthed her baby, another princess for the palace. Morning broke with the first breathe of newborn coming into the world. Little Hatice was a joy, and Mara loved holding her. Serving Stella through the birth had been a privilege.

Singing to the baby, playing with the children, painting, writing calligraphy, and helping with the household filled Mara's days. She hummed and carried Peace with her where she went, and the women, even Ayla, had all come to trust her as someone who would not gossip or suspect anyone of ill intent.

Mara was painting near the fountain when the Head Eunuch announced that the banner of the Sultan had been seen cresting the hill. Everyone dropped what they were doing and rushed to get ready. Thus all were gathered to greet him with the honor due his name when he arrived.

Emine and Halime Hâtûn were with him too. It was a great returning home, and the welcomes were all about. But Mara was disappointed to see that the Sultan was still angry and carrying frustration. She wished she could solve it.

It was Emine Hâtûn who pulled her aside almost immediately to inform her of the news. Apparently her brothers had been found plotting against the Sultan and siding with Hunyadi in Europe. Her brother Grgur had been imprisoned in Amasya and was now officially blinded as a result of his lack of loyalty[48]. Emine Hâtûn was angry, and felt justified in reflected the Sultan's anger. Mara's family were traitors and were to be viewed with contempt.

This news struck Mara like a sword to her soul. She did not know if she was more heartbroken that the Sultan could do this to her own brother or if she was heartbroken that this conquest of Europe was unjust in the first place. Neither did she have the time to ponder what her own thoughts on the matter might be. These were of no import. The fact was, she was related to the offender.

With two of his sons dead and former allies fighting him to the east and west, the Sultan was wary and frustrated.

"You and your family are traitors," Emine Hâtûn said firmly, "for this reason, you will pack your bags immediately. You are being sent, under guard, to Edirne. You are being banished. Your family is not trustworthy."

Mara felt a buzzing in her head, and Emine's last sentence felt like it was coming at her from a distant corridor. She steadied herself. Forcing her mind back into the moment she bowed slightly before Emine Hâtûn.

"I am sorry, Emine Hâtûn," she whispered, "you know I am loyal. I will do as you bid."

Emine Hâtûn spun on her heels and left the room, stopping only to add, "be ready by morning. Your ride leaves at dawn."

Mara sunk to the floor, on her knees. She raised her hands to her Father in Heaven. Tears ran down her cheeks.

"Papa," she cried, "I tried so hard. I'm sorry."

At once she felt God's enveloping Presence and heard His whisper in her spirit.

"You did, child. All will be well."

His Peace galvanized her. She looked around the small room that had been her chamber all these years. It shook her to imagine leaving, but she felt Holy Spirit blow gently, and realized that she loved adventure, and travel, and that she could choose to enjoy this. She felt the Lord confirm His Peace in her. She had done all she could do. This was not her fault.

Standing slowly she began to gather her things.

Part III:

The Banishment

The route north-west to Edirne was a balm to Mara's soul. All of creation seemed to match her sorrow. Sheets of rain beat upon the carriage. Several times they were forced to stop and extract a wheel from the mud. Twice they had to go around a flooded zone.

In the brief interludes between rain, mists rose from sodden fields and copses. Winds whipped at the few remaining leaves on scattered trees.

When a scant period of clear skies brought reprieve, the heavens were full of birds, going as one, in the very opposite direction Mara was being taken. Flamingoes and storks, geese and starlings all strained south, while she was being driven north.

The ruts in the roads were deep and the constant, unpredictable jolts and bumps were tiring. Knowing that they would eventually travel by boat across the Marmara was small comfort. It was autumn, and the waters tended to roughen this time of year. It was not for nothing the Sultan and retinue had returned home to Bursa ahead of winter storms.

Mara sighed. "Papa," she prayed, "You said all will be well. I know You always speak Truth and I can trust You, but this is hard. I can't hardly grasp that Grgur is in prison, blinded. Blinded! Sightless! How cruel! Never to see Vuk again!"

Mara fell silent and sensed that Jesus wept with her. This surprised her for a moment, and then spoke to her heart. She fingered the key necklace. This evil was not from God. Evil came from evil, good came from God. When her thoughts flew to the why of it, the answer came just as swiftly. "A tree is known by its fruit[49]."

"Yes," she realized in her heart. "I've become accustomed to the ways of the

Muslims, living amongst them, but the fruit of the tree is consistent."

How Mara wished there was someone who could explain what was really going on! For many of the girls in the Harem, the outside world held no interest. But she was a political pawn, and was being banished for events that had taken place on the other side of the board!

A shaft of light broke through storm clouds to her left. It fell on a hamlet in the distance, far enough away to be silent and picturesque, even if the people in it may have led tempestuous lives. Again Mara sensed the whisper of the Lord in her spirit.

Abdiya Wesab

She had been obedient to His Call on her life. She had made it possible for her people to live in peace. Her father's realm was full of villages where women and girls were safe because of her personal sacrifice. Papa God was pleased with her, but not pleased with the situation. He hadn't created the conflict with the Ottomans, He didn't endorse it, He wept over it. But He was pleased with her response in the situation.

"Peace," Mara felt the whisper. She had carried peace into the Harem, and her Peace was traveling with her now. That cheered her. She did not need to give in to the condemnations that Emine Hâtûn and the Sultan had heaped upon her. Gently fingering her necklace she felt memories of her time in Bursa wash over her.

Suddenly Mara realized that the Sultan had behaved like a spoiled child. He couldn't control the war, Europe, or the people in the territories he wanted to conquer, but he could control Mara, so he had lashed out at her. Somehow that realization gave her compassion for him. Poor man, he was caught in a religion that dictated that he had to conquer the world. What a weight to carry on one's shoulders!

A flock of geese lifted off the water they were passing. Their lilting, wild cries sang the song Mara was feeling. She remembered the day, a few weeks earlier, that she had overseen the plucking and preparation of a flock of domestic geese. As Emine Hâtûn had charged them, the *Kadın* had been busy preparing for Ramadan. Mara smiled. Ahhhh, this meant that she would miss Ramadan. How wonderful! Although she had served the household faithfully through many-a month of fasting, she was grateful. Ramadan was a heavy month, spiritually, with so many do's and don't, and so many people self flagellating to prove themselves to Allah that it got wearisome.

She felt Papa God smile with her. Suddenly she realized that, although the Sultan meant this season to be a punishment, it was up to her what she did with it. And with that she sat straight up. "Advent!" she almost shouted, "Advent and Christmas!"

It was well that Mara had something she set herself to take Joy in. Her welcome in Edirne was cold. She was the only woman in the Harem. The servants of the palace were on maintenance mode. They kicked into high gear if and when the Sultan came. But otherwise, everything was quiet, and these in between times were used to work their own lands, and fill their larders.

Mara stood at the window and took stock of the situation. She was essentially in solitary confinement. Most certainly there were a few butlers and eunuchs, cooks and scullery maids about the place, but she was the only inmate of the

Harem. Worse still, it was apparent from the behavior of all she met that she was to be treated with contempt as a traitor. Not only was she an infidel, she was perhaps in cahoots with the Europeans beyond the river and was not to be trusted.

"Well, Papa," she said, sitting down in the cold window seat, "it's good that I know who I am in Christ, and that I have been faithful. With a pure conscience I can choose to view this new season as an appeal for Advent; an appeal for Your Appearing. How deeply the world needs Emmanuel is shouting at me from this silence."

It was very nearly pointless to try and even look out the window. A frost had settled, hoary and white, drawing ferns across the opaque glass. For a moment Mara smiled, remembering breathing on the window as a child, and peeking through the hole. She did so again, gaining a rather stark view of her environment.

The land was undulating, with an orchard set in solid rows. A few scraggly pears and apples clung to the scant trees. Magpies seemed the only moving creature alive and content to be about in the frost.

Sighing, Mara turned back and looked at the room. But for the light from the window and the fire on the hearth, there was little to cheer her. But she stood and put her hands on her hips.

Abdiya Wesab

"Papa, the Magi had to choose to leave their safe palaces to set out and seek you. The journey was arduous. They were not sure what they would find. That was their journey through Advent as we know it now. I have become perhaps too accustomed to being cocooned in the relative safety of many women and children. We've been hovered over and given anything one might have a whim for, entertained endlessly, and I've whittled away years of my life in that small circle. I sense …"she went a stood by the fire, warming her hands. "I sense that You are preparing me for something. This is a new season. What the Sultan has done in anger, You will use for my good."

She listened in her heart for a minute and smiled.

"Yes. You are giving me the beginning of the answer to my request to be able to be celibate and serve You. Here I will have no distractions. I have my calligraphy pen and ink, I have my paints and paper, I have the sections of the Word of God that I copied out earlier. I will translate the Scriptures I have with me! This would be a delight. If I ever get to go back to Bursa, I can share them with Ertine. Maybe Stella will be ready to receive them as well."

Mara's choice to be content, and write calligraphy intrigued the staff. They were accustomed to women who were demanding and made their wishes known. Mara hummed to herself while she worked, oblivious to the fact that the household found her curious.

Mara's days took on a rhythm. She chose to set herself a schedule. Waking early, she would worship the Lord before sun up. After a small repast, she set to work, translating and writing. Mid-morning she stopped to tidy and clean, giving her eyes, mind and body a break. This was also when the occasional maid came sweeping in the court yard, collecting waste, or shaking rugs. It gave her a moment to talk with another human, for which she was grateful. That she personally cleaned her own space was a surprise to them.

Mara Ḫâtûn

In the afternoons Mara once again curled up with her work. Occasionally sunlight blessed her, slanting through the orchard on its descent down the sky. She praised God that in this palace she had a window to the outside world. What a delight that was! By dusk she was ready to stretch again. Wandering by the silent and empty pools of the Harem reminded her of her loneliness, but she chose to not let it affect her spirit.

Meals had been being delivered to Mara on trays with a rap on the door. One afternoon she decided to explore the extent of her boundaries and find out if perhaps there were little ways she might help in the kitchen.

Following her nose, she found the scullery, with a great fire place. A tiny fire had been built in one corner of it to keep the chill off. In a stone abode the damp even came through the walls if heat was not present in some way.

She knocked gently on the partially open door so as to not startle anyone. An older woman turned with a "who's there?"

When she saw Mara she took her hands out of the bread she was kneading and placed them on her wide hips.

"Excuse me," Mara said politely, "it's rather boring all alone in my room. Back in Bursa I used to help in the kitchen. Is there anything I can do to help you?"

Mara Hâtûn

The cook seemed a little taken aback. She knew how to handle a houseful of *Kadın* and *Gözde*. She had seen Emine Hâtûn order the lesser beings to assist here and there, but it had always been against their will, and beneath their station. This was a strange one, offering to help.

"Well," she hesitated, "I don't see why not. There's not a lot to do, really, with just a few of us rattling around in this great place, but we do all eat, and I occasionally put some things away for the next season."

She looked Mara up and down, "you seem strong enough. Here, want to knead the dough? My arms have had enough to be sure!"

Abdiya Wesab

Mara smiled and gladly went at it. It was a very pleasant reprieve from her solitary confinement. Deftly moving the dough in the roll, kneed, punch, turn, she introduced herself.

The cook was surprised again. Fancy someone wanting to know her name. No one had ever asked her that here.

"I'm Nora," she answered simply, "but I'm mostly called Cook."

"Have you always lived in Edirne?" Mara asked.

"No, my people are from over across the river a ways," Nora responded, "I was taken as a slave and sold into the palace. It's a better life than many have, I suppose."

Mara nodded. She didn't want to pry. Such a strange economy war created, uprooting people and making them subjects of another realm.

The bread was ready. "Shall I make flat bread or shape it?" she asked.

"Some of both," Nora responded. She was scrubbing carrots and celery roots now.

"Lovely looking vegetables!" Mara commented. "are they from the palace gardens or grown nearby?"

"This vicinity is fair famous for these," Nora held a fat celery root up. "The palace gardens were scant this year. The river washed over its banks a little too high. But the market provided what we need."

"You've certainly mastered Turkish well!" Mara said.

"Yours isn't bad either!" Nora smiled. Her grin revealed several missing teeth, but this became her somehow. Mara felt that she had a softness hidden behind the strong shoulders and busy demeanor.

It proved to be true. After that, Mara found a way to help out a bit almost every day. It did her good to take a break from writing, and she was extremely grateful that she hadn't been put in full solitary confinement. Not that she said anything or asked questions. The men about the place seemed austere and militant in nature and she was glad that she didn't need to interact with them. She only ever saw them from a distance, if there was a clatter of hooves in the circle drive when she was working in the kitchen. For once she was thankful for the security of the Harem, and the station she carried.

The only man she ever really saw was the very old and wizened black eunuch who had been left behind to watch over the place. He had been stern and given her orders when she first arrived. But when he saw how compliant and gentle she was he softened and gradually very nearly ignored her. He had a spot in the sun at the opposite end of the Harem. He sat just outside, with the keys, at the entrance. Here he had his cushions and his *nargile*. pipe. Nora said that he slept most of the time.

It was Nora who reminded her when they reached the shortest day of the year. "Back in my village we used to plant Christmas Wheat," she said, fondly, "it was meant to grow through Advent until Christmas. Then we put a candle in the middle."

"We did too!" Mara exclaimed, "and we children would ask Mother for soaked kernels of wheat. They were such fun to chew. Especially once they grew their roots out."

Mara Hâtûn

"In our village we would light candles to remember Saint Lucia too."

"Yes, and my mother would bake special bread!"

"Lucia was a brave girl," Nora nodded, "yes, my life's been hard, but I've not been burnt at the stake."

They were husking and sorting beans together. The cheerful ker-plunk of beans gathering in tin pans filled their moments of shared silence. Mara was thoughtful.

"What did you do at Christmas, then?" she asked.

Nora smiled, remembering. "My parents were good folks. They made sure we knew the difference between traditions and Truth. Round about Michaelmas other girls would put out garlic to ward off the werewolves and our family would light candles for Advent. We always fasted for the six weeks leading to Christmas. How about you?"

"Yes, we did too. Our fast was just from meat, eggs and dairy, though. It was always so exciting to begin looking forward to Christmas and preparing for it while we fasted!" Mara agreed.

"Yes, we would make round bread, and share it with our neighbors. Did you?" Nora asked.

"Yes," Mara said, remembering, "I'll make some this year, if you will let me. It would be fun to celebrate some of the old traditions!"

"Yes! Lets!" Nora agreed, "it's just you and me here, anyhow. The few servants come and go, and won't be here at Christmas. And we can give the Eunuch some as well. I'm sure he'd be glad of something special to eat!"

While she and Nora had fun creating new memories around old traditions, the highlight of Mara's Christmas was being able to sing Christmas worship and not worry that she was bothering anyone. She lit candles and took time with Jesus. She felt His love, and, when she felt

Abdiya Wesab

lonely she touched her necklace and
remembered her family in prayer.

Over and over she found her heart
singing:

Creator of the starry height,
Thy people's everlasting light,
Jesu, Redeemer, save us all,
Hear thou thy servants when they call.
Thou, sorrowing at the helpless cry
Of all creation doomed to die,
Didst save our lost and guilty race
By healing gifts of heavenly grace.

When earth was near its evening hour,
Thou didst, in love's redeeming power,
Like bridegroom from his chamber,
come
Forth from a Virgin-mother's womb.

Mara Hâtûn

At thy great Name, exalted now,
All knees in lowly homage bow;
All things in heaven and earth adore,
And own Thee King for evermore.

To thee, O Holy One, we pray,
Our Judge in that tremendous day,
Ward off, while yet we dwell below,
The weapons of our crafty foe.
To God the Father, God the Son,
And God the Spirit, Three in One,
Praise, honor, might and glory be
From age to age eternally[50].

Mara realized afresh that her moments of worship were a gift of time she could never have had if she had been in Bursa. During that season with the other women and children she had always been available for everyone around her. Now she had time to simply soak in the Word of God and listen to His heart. She felt His Presence draw her closer and she took delight in Him.

In the time between the years, after Christmas and before New Years, Nora and Mara counted out the days until Epiphany. The kitchen opened onto the garden and orchard. Just beyond these a stone wall encased the palace and was framed by the main road, which approached them from a rise. This gave them instant notice of any approaching carriages. Thus when an entourage of the Sultan's men arrived for an overnight stay, Mara saw them arrive from the kitchen, but was very grateful to disappear into the shadows of the

Harem and know that she was virtually invisible before they arrived.

The shouting about and orders echoing through the courtyard made Mara aware that these were not just ordinary nobodies. She was grateful that her room was in the farthest corner of the Harem. For some unknown reason, these men made her feel uneasy. Almost not safe. For the first time she bolted her door.

To her surprise she found that there was suddenly a flurry of sound on the other side of her wall. At first she was confused. Then she realized that the men's quarters buttressed right up to the back of her chamber.

"Ah, well, I can put up with a little noise," she thought, "I'm getting quite spoiled having this place all to myself."

There was scrapping and banging about. Mara deduced that furniture had been arranged to serve a meal. This proved true when she heard the clatter of dishes and the grunts of the men as they settled upon the divan, right up against her wall.

Mara settled down with her calligraphy. She was five chapters into the letter which the Apostle Paul had written to the church in Rome. Such a fascinating Epistle! She had reached verse fifteen:

"But the gift is not like the trespass. For if the many died by the trespass of the one man, how much more did God's grace and the gift that came by the grace of the one man, Jesus Christ, overflow to the many! Nor can the gift of God be compared with the result of one man's sin: The judgment followed one sin and brought condemnation, but the gift followed many trespasses and brought justification. For if, by the trespass of the one man, death reigned through that one man, how much more will those who receive God's abundant provision of grace and of the gift of righteousness reign in life through the one man, Jesus Christ!"

Gradually Mara became aware that the men on the other side of the wall were talking. At first she didn't tune in. Then she heard them mention her father's name, Đurađ Branković. She froze.

Abdiya Wesab

Setting her ink and pen carefully aside she crept over to the wall and put her ear to it. These men knew her father?

"The Sultan will do what I suggest," one voice muttered. He took a long draught and let out a sigh. "He knows full well it is up to him to destroy the enemies of our faith. Allah has given him this vast domain. I've told him that if he continues to show Allah disdain by enfolding these infidels in benevolent forbearance Allah will remove blessings from him[51]."

The other man's voice was shriller and more nasal. He scraped a metal utensil against a dish. "I agree. This cannot be the will of Allah. The Sultan must consume the flesh of the impious until they revert to the teaching of the one Allah and his great Prophet, peace be upon him."

"This is why the works of Đurađ Branković are so despicable," the first voice responded, chewing while he talked, "I know that the Sultan granted him permission to build Smederevo[52], and that it was meant to be a fortress on those northern reaches of the Ottoman dynasty[53]. But the man used it for his own gain and will do so again. Bide my words!"

"Besides," the nasal voice agreed, slurping what sounded to be soup, "it is strategically placed to enable us to cross over into Hungary. Benevolent Fazlullah, you do well to push your case."

Mara very nearly held her breath, listening. Dark was falling, but she didn't bother to light a lamp, remaining silently up against the wall. She clasped the key about her neck and prayed.

"There is also the other issue, my Ansar," Fazlullah retorted, "Our problem is Çandarlı Halil Pasha. While he remains an advisor to the Sultan, our approach against the infidel will remain cordial and slow. But every tract of land we gain in the Balkans advances the goals of Allah and dominion of the world for Shari'a. Halil Pasha is old and soft."

"He does not value the lining of the Sultan's coffers as you so wisely do. Neither will he be hard to get rid of," the nasal voice said softly, "you are the *defterdar*[54] of the Sublime Porte, your wisdom is my command."

Lord Fazlullah sounded confident, "you will find an opportune moment, then?"

"To be sure I will. A well aimed arrow always hits its mark. Just as you so tactfully brought Saruca to public shame at the waning of summer."

Lord Fazlullah laughed a cold and calculated snicker. Then he clapped his hands.

The sound startled Mara and she drew away from the wall in horror. Should the

Sultan be warned somehow about these men?

"That was brilliant!" she head him go on, "Saruca served the Sultan as his *mukarrrib*[55], but his religious advise proved to be a fallacy. It was his strategy that allowed that fool daughter of Đurađ Branković to be used as a contractual bridge in the first place. It was time to shame him before the Sultan and point out that he was allowing an infidel sipahi's[56] daughter to usurp the rightful place that only the daughters of true Muslims should enjoy."

Mara gasped. So the Sultan hadn't sent her away in mere anger. There was fouler play at work than she knew. Whoever these men in the next room were, it was to be hoped that they didn't know she was here! Silently she began praying. She asked for angelic protection and to be kept in the Shadow of the Almighty. She also prayed for her father's protection.

"At this pace, we should be in Bursa by Ramadan," the nasal voice rejoined, pausing for a drink, "there is much to be done."

"Do not forget how willing Saruca is to take a bribe. Me thinks this is why he has proven so disloyal to our People of the Faith. Smederevo was a lie. Đurađ Branković was given permission to build a church for his sniveling peasants. Of course he turned it into a fortress! This way he could plan war against our people. It would not surprise me if

Saruca cajoled money out of Đurađ Branković's hand itself."

"How little these men know," Mara thought to herself. She had been there when her father and the Sultan had brokered the agreement about Smederevo. Her father had only requested permission to build a monastery. The Sultan had advised him to make it a fortress. It stood the Sultan in good stead to use peasant labor to build him a loyal fortress on the border of Hungary.

"My Lord Fazulullah," the nasal voice went on, "you are *Deftardar* in the company of Viziers to the Sultan. Yes, others on this counsel include Saruca and Halil Candarli, but you are the most wise and cunning, who uses the *Makr* of

Allah[57] to advance the purposes of the Sultan. Allah will give you favor when you stand before the Sultan."

"It is also helpful to remember that it was but recently that King Sigismund of Hungary ordered his men march through Đurađ Branković's land to attack us. If Branković was loyal, he would have ordered them out[58]."

"Exactly. He would have joined forces against Sigismund in defense of the Ottomans."

"But no, he and his ilk are not to be trusted. It was well that we called them out and held them responsible."

"And it will continue to play into our hands," the nasal one droned on, "even though the report came through that Đurađ had not given Sigismund the permission, it stands in the records against him. We will use it well, going forward."

"Besides," Fazulullah agreed, "with two of his sons blinded his posterity is all but useless. This will work out well for the conquest of these infidels and the promotion of the People of the Faith."

Mara was not sure she could take any more. Two brothers blind? Two? She forced herself to continue as third party to this parlay. Tears streamed down her face, but she realized that the Lord was letting her know things that she needed to know.

"I predict a northern invasion in the spring, my Lord, if you have your way!" laughed the nasal one.

"Quite naturally, my Ansar, my disciple," Fazulullah sounded pleased with himself, "learn well. So are won the wars of men[59]!"

Mara moved away from the wall, to the opposite end of the room, fearful that she might make a sound. She stifled her tears and covered her face with her scarf to hide the sobs.

"What am I to do with this, Lord?" She asked.

Book II

In the second volume of Mara Hâtûn the answer to Mara's question will unfold. Unexpected fruit will be Harvested.

You will unravel the mystery of Yusuf Adil, Sultan of Bijapur, India, meet the next two Sultans of the Ottoman Empire, and get to know the women who held their hearts. And yes, Mahtab Hâtûn will surface again as well, this time with a princess.

A certain Rabbi will emerge as an unexpected link to a brighter future, and the key will unlock the prevention of a massacre[60].

Mara Hâtûn

Appendix

Understanding
Ottoman governance & structure:

As with every government, over time the Ottoman Empire took shape. It had several facets unique to its people and worldview. Some of these are explained here, others will have become apparent as you read this book.

Earlier Turkic tribes, the sons of Osman included, were led more by elders and religious men. Seniority and tenure was respected. Osman, for instance, took only two wives, and both of them were daughters of men he respected and worked with, men who believed in him, and spent time with him.

The Sultan was the ruler. He yielded the sword of Allah, and felt it to be his responsibility to fulfill the commands of Muhammed to conquer the world so that peace could come when all of mankind submitted to Islam under Shari'a law. Thus the sons of Sultans were reared to fight and rule. This was so integral to the fiber of their beings that they first had to prove themselves capable of ruling provincially, and serve in conquest, then, once their father died, they had to each fight each other for the throne. The words "successor" and "conflict" have the same root in Arabic[61]. Each son was given to a tutor early on to prepare him for a fight to the death where the fittest and wittiest won.

To rule the Sublime Porte, as his throne was named, the Sultan had a counsel or *Divan* comprised of viziers and advisors. The *vezir-i azam* was the Grand Vizier. The Lord of the European provinces, also called the *Beylerbey* of Rumelia was also on the counsel. Sometimes a third vizier was appointed, depending on the favor of the Sultan. The Sultan's team also included the *Kazasker*, or chief military judge, the *Defterdar*, or finance minister, and the *Nişancı*, or keeper of the imperial monogram. This last was also scribe and calligrapher.

Abdiya Wesab

As the Ottomans moved from being one tribe among many to The tribe which gave the world a Sultan to wield the Sword of Muhammed, the men who ruled directly under the Sultan were no longer wise, older men with a rich cultural heritage in the ways of their forefathers. The Divan became a place where power was a delicate chess game and Viziers lost their heads and positions as easily as a slave might. The game went both ways. Men of the Divan also learned how to manipulate the Sultan.

Intrigue was not relegated solely to the male members of the Sultans retinue. The Harem was perhaps intended to be an earthly replica of the Muslim's concept of paradise. Women were abundant, and the Sultan might have any he set eyes on. In fact, the Sultan's mother was tasked with sorting out the women tithed to him. She selected and groomed them and then arranged them as *Gözde*, or those whom his eye might fall upon, always within view. It should perhaps not surprise us that this, and other complications, made this Paradise a little less than heavenly.

Understanding Slavery in the Ottoman Empire:

Taking territory and with it slaves, was expected. Islam must advance by the sword or allegiances. The later was less preferred, but sufficient as a means to open a door into a new region. Practice had shown them that if they entered through allegiance, with time, they would conquer that land. Such contracts were crafted to push those they threatened to choose the lesser of two evils. Typically the Sultan demanded a woman of the royal family in exchange for relative peace. This was a political marriage and it is not known if the Sultan always consummated these relationships. His Harem was full of many other women who had ambitions and made their presence known.

Slavery was normative and carefully outlined in Shari'a law[62]. The terms were clear: slaves might only be taken from non-Muslim territories. The Arab trade in slaves had served the frontline of battle since the inception of Islam, and by the 800s they were being bought from Africa to use in warfare[63].

Once an area came under Muslim rule, surviving non-Muslims could opt to retain "freedom of religion" if they paid the *jaziyah or jizya* or capitation tax. As long as they kept up their regular payments, they could maintain their religion, and were assigned to a specific region to live in. They came under assigned governance, were limited in what they could do and where they could go, and their word had half the value of a Muslim in a court of law. One in five of their sons was tithed to the Sultan. Called *devshirme* in Turkish , '*paedomazoma*', or 'collection of children' in Greek; '*tribut de sânge*' in Romanian; '*danak u krvi*' in Serbian, and '*kraven danak*' or 'blood tax' in Bulgarian, this taxation spread wherever the Ottoman Empire conquered. Also should a

Muslim so much as see one of their daughters and ask for her, there was no refusing him. These "free" people lived in what were called "millets."

From the Muslim perspective, if a non-Muslim captive people didn't pay the *jizya* protection and subjugation tax, those people were considered at war with the Muslim *umma*, or nation. The tax was ensured through enslaving those people. By setting the *jizya* high, these situations were easily manipulated to the profit of the conquering horde. In contrast, in parts of Africa proselytizing was refrained from, because it might reduce the potential stream of slaves[64].

Long before the conquest of Constantinople, Muslim cities had organized slave markets, handling slaves of all ages, and both sexes as chattel, selling them naked so they could be checked by buyers[65]. In northeastern Africa it was customary for the value of female slaves to increase if they were made unable to conceive[66]. It took until the colonization of Somalia to end this. The practice of the slave markets was also ended by colonization, although tribal slavery continued to surface until the 1930s[67].

Conditions en route to market were harsh as well. 80,000 slaves were estimated to die annually before arriving at any one of African's port market[68]. Arab authors recorded the details of slave markets as part of their travel experience. Authors such as Al-Bakri, author of *Kitāb al-Masālik wa'l-Mamālik* or Book of Roads and Kingdoms, published in Córdoba around 1068, gives information and collected eye-witness accounts on Saharan caravan routes. Ibn Battuta, who lived until about 1377, was a Muslim Moroccan geographer who travelled sub-Saharan Africa, including Gao and Timbuktu. He wrote 'A Gift to Those Who Contemplate the Wonders of Cities and the Marvels of Traveling' His commentaries include personal realities, such as being given a boy-child slave as a gift of hospitality. Rifa'a al-Tahtawi wrote similarly about North Africa until 1873.

In 1814 Swiss explorer Johann Burckhardt travelled in Africa and encountered the realities of the eastern slave markets. He was appalled that the general practice was so indecent that rape was even laughed at[69]. David Livingstone travelled the African Great Lakes in the mid-nineteenth century, and wrote of slavery: "To overdraw its evils is a simple impossibility ... We passed a slave woman shot or stabbed through the body and lying on the path. [Onlookers] said an Arab who passed early that morning had done it in anger at losing the price he had given for her, because she was unable to walk any longer. We passed a woman tied by the neck to a tree and dead ... We came upon a man dead from starvation ... The strangest disease I have seen in this country seems really to be broken heartedness, and it attacks free men who have been captured and made slaves[70]."

Livingstone was so appalled that he turned his attention to exposing and communicating about the realities of the slave trade over and above his former goals of exploration[71].

Should someone convert to Islam, he had the benefits of being on the winning side. Slavery had a caste system of sorts. Male slaves taken in war or by piracy were charged to convert. Should they do so manumission was encouraged. These and the boys taken in tithe were called "*kul*" and could work their way up in rank, often achieving status in the military. Those who proved themselves could end up ruling lands under order of the Sultan. Eventually high ranking officers, ministers of government, and commanders were staffed by *kul*. The staff in the palace, the entire Janissary Corps and all the Sultan's calvary were men who were *kul*. Because of the offices they held, there were free Muslims who obeyed these men, even though they were technically slaves in the sense of being *kul*. These *kul* received salaries, but no inheritance. They did eventually develop ways to have a united political voice in some situations, but they were never not subservient to and owned by the Sultan. Their heads were ever expendable, and their positions eliminated at whim.

Slaves in the true sense of the word existed as well. Some of these were forced to become eunuchs and were called *hadım*. The concept of making slave boys eunuchs was also ancient, but expanded under the Muslim slave trade. They could be marketed as guards to the harems and holy sites[72]. This 'honor' befell them if they excelled in studies and were not deemed fit for service as Janissary, who were the at the forefront of the Sultan's wars. In fact, Arab slave traders developed an exclusive and elite slave market of both black and white boys who underwent the forced surgery to get the highest price from the Sultan's coffers[73]. None of the eunuchs were ever Turkish, or Muslim, for Islam forbade Muslims from castrating their own, neither was a Muslim allowed by Islam to do this nasty work. The evil task was done by others, under duress, and could be claimed to simply be the kismet of those to whom it was done. Whereas in places like China and Persia it was historically customary and one would find native eunuchs, the source countries for those enslaved by Muslims as eunuchs were non-Muslim[74]. By the time Mehmed was Sultan there were at least forty such men serving in the palace[75].

Most male slaves were simply that. Typical work for Ottoman slaves of every race included being chained to ships as rowers, driven to quarries, carrying ivory in long *calibants*, chained together, or sold in market for hard labor. It is estimated that only 6% of slaves survived the long march to market. Chained as they were, if one man tired, he was beheaded, to not stop the *calibant*[76]. It was clear that any man who didn't have the sense to become a

Muslim was a fool to 'choose' to become enslaved.

Whereas prior to the dawn of the Ottoman Empire intercontinental slave markets had been limited to the Arab capture and sale of mostly Africans men to serve as fodder for Islamic armies, once Islam grew to the status of Empire slavery was highly profitable.

By 696 the Caliphs of Arabia were using African slaves as soldiers. By the ninth century the Arab Sultanate of Zanzibar captured Bantu people, using Swahili traders[77]. Islamic invasions of India also took hundreds of thousands from the region. Within a short time the slave trade was profiting from tens of thousands of Bantu and shipping increased to the Persian Gulf, India, Egypt, and the Horn of Africa[78]. An uprising of African slaves[79] in Iraq from 869 to 883 involved over 500,000 slaves who had been imported and brought for agricultural work[80]. Between the 8th and 19th century at least 18 million people were bought from local slave traders in Africa and taken across the Red Sea, Indian Ocean and the Sahara desert towards the eastern markets.

The Arab slave trade of Africans had initially been limited to an act of conquest. Slaves taken in war were offered as a human sacrifice[81]. Now slavery increased for profit, and tribes were pitted against each other to procure fresh slaves from the interior for profit. Likewise Muslims took to piracy in coastal Africa and Europe so violently that whole towns were abandoned as people escaped to the interior. This trade was prolific as far north as Iceland, Scotland and England[82] and at least 700 Americans were taken as Muslim pirates boarded ships traveling to Europe[83]. This was an efficient and approved method of conquest, because anyone who converted to Islam was set free[84]. It is estimated that the slave market in Constantinople alone processed about 2.5 million slaves from 1450 to 1700[85]. The Ottoman practice of killing the men and taking female and child captives as they conquered Europe was galling. Raids as late as 1769 were still taking 20,000 captives at a time[86].

Mara Ḫâtûn

In Europe several religious orders were started with the goal to ransom Christian slaves, provide hospitals for those who were suffering, and meet the needs of widows and orphans who had been left bereft as a result of these raids[87]. In 1785 Thomas Jefferson and John Adams even went to London to try and negotiate free passage by sea. They met with Tripoli's envoy, Ambassador Sidi Haji Abdrahaman. But he defended his right to take slaves, saying it was "founded on the Laws of the Prophet, that it was written in their Koran that all nations who should not have answered their authority were sinners, that it was their right and duty to make war upon them wherever they could be found, and to make slaves of all they could take as prisoners, and that every Mussulman who should be slain in battle was sure to go to Paradise[88]". Eventually, even the United States paid tribute to them in order to stave off attacks of their ships[89].

This ended with the Barbary wars, when the United States, Britain, Netherlands and France formed an alliance and fought until the Barbary pirates were crushed. The demand for white slaves in the market was huge, so the forced agreement to terminate slave taking was only temporarily staved when the pirate fleets were immobilized. But the pirates restructured. It took putting Algiers and Tunis under French colonial rule to make the seas safe to travel. Slave traders finally met justice. European governments passed laws that gave emancipation to slaves[90]. Although this did not terminate or stave the demand for slaves in the east, it ended piracy and Western Europeans being taken in slavery.

To draw a comparison of an individual leader, it could be added that although men like Christopher Columbus took slaves from South and Central America, and was discovered to have treated some tribes harshly, when the King and Queen of Spain learned of his behavior he was removed from office and imprisoned for doing this[91]. Also to draw a comparison of a nation, we can look at the slave trade which was exported to America.

Prior to 1705 blacks and whites alike went to the "New World" as indentured servants, a position they could work themselves out from under. While there are reports of slavers coming to Virginia with slaves, and other slave traders taking Native Americans captive, it was not accepted, condoned, or even widely known until later.

The Virginia Slave Codes of 1705 legitimized slavery in the colonies and it remained a blight on the nation until the Republican Party introduced the 13th Amendment into Congress. The 160 years in between are a shame to that nation. In the horrific slave trade of this specific era about 10.5 million people arrived as slaves in the Americas. It is estimated that another 4 million died en-route to the ships, and about 1.5 million died on board the slave ships[92]. This horror of human history is dark and morbid, and should never have been. But true Christians challenged this until it changed, and slavery and its remnant consequences have repeatedly been addressed and repented for at the initiative of American citizens who are appalled at this aspect of its history, whereas those who remain true to the Quran continue to take slaves to this day[93].

Prior to Ottoman slavery, any conquering tribe anywhere had taken slaves, from Britain to China, South Africa to South America. Slavery was a global blight which was normalized by sinful human nature.

Early slavery was sometimes even a personal choice. Some societies had codified rules for length and terms of service. The Old Testament law included details about this. Although people could be and were taken in captive in war, if someone had a debt to pay, they could sell themselves into slavery to pay the debt through labor, and then regain their liberty. Even slaves taken in war had rights of manumission. In Rome, a slave was freed in a ceremony where the *praetor* touched the slave with a rod called a *vindicta,* pronouncing him free. The word *vindicta* is where English gets its word vindication. The slave's head was shaved and a *pileus* was placed upon it. Both the *vindicta* and the cap were considered symbols of liberty[94]. A freed slave was now a citizen, and had the right to vote.

Mara Ḥâtûn

In Constantinople itself, in 316AD Constantine added another way to legally free a slave: you could go to a church and use the bishop as your witness, whereupon they were now free Roman citizens. He applied these laws to both men and women[95]. But under the Ottoman rule in Constantinople, the slave market was so vast that they had a guild of 2,000 to run it[96]. In Ottoman Constantinople, jobs pertaining to vice were relegated to the "infidels". It was understood that the the assigned task of the Greeks was to keep the taverns, the Armenians were to be money changers, and the Jews those who arranged for prostitution or 'amorous intrigues[97].' The Jews were also assigned the task of managing the slave markets in Constantinople, and as infidels, had no choice but to do what they were told to do. From the 15th century on, Constantinople became the hub of the slave trade. By then, more slaves were being provided by the Tatar raids, which continued until the Crimean war in the late 18th century. At least two million slaves came through their sourcing alone. Thus Constantinople's markets had three streams: the Barbary trade, the African markets and European conquest[98].

For women slaves the situation was simpler. They were more vulnerable in war, especially because the Quran detailed how Muslim soldiers had the right to use them as concubines[99]. After the top most beautiful were tithed to the Sultan, superfluous females went to market. This included little girls.

But under the Ottomans slavery was systemized and racism developed. When the Sultan's conquering hordes sorted out those women to tithe[100], women with paler skin became those most qualified for the Sultan's Harem. Because the Sultan used the women in his Harem to award his best men, white women became prized, and darker women were relegated to lesser value. Although the Sultan eventually ruled North Africa, African women were never part of the Harem and he never allowed his royal blood to mingle racially[101]. This reality did not become obvious to the rest of the world until the Crimean war, when the glut of Circassian women on the market so lowered their price in the slave trade of Constantinople, that news articles commented on this fact[102]. Men were bringing their darker skinned slaves and concubines to market and trading them in, as if they were stock.

The eunuchs which served in the Harem were called *Sandali*, and would be appointed to serve in the harem. The Chief Black Eunuch was called the *Kizlar Agha*, or Ruler of the Girls. He was the only male who entered the harem. His roles included protecting the women, choosing which new *Odalisque* went to the Sultan's bedchamber, going to market and purchasing new slaves to train as *Odalisques*, and overseeing the hierarchy of the women and the minor eunuchs. He was a witness in the event that a Sultan did choose to marry a *Kadin*, he was present for birth ceremonies, and arranged all the royal circumcision parties. He also was responsible to manage those women accused of crimes, taking them to the executioner, where they were put into sacks and drowned in the Bosphorus[103].

Lest we relegate this to history, currently popular Muslim preacher Abu Ishaq al-Huwaini goes to great lengths to justify Muslims in their conquest and selling of conquered infidel women. As he said, "When I want a sex-slave, I go to the market and pick whichever female I desire and buy her[104]." Political activist and former parliamentary candidate for Kuwait's government, Salwa al-Mutairi is a woman. She justifies the institution of sex-slavery. As she points out, "A Muslim state must first attack a Christian state—sorry, I mean any non-Muslim state—and they [the women, the future sex-slaves] must be captives of the raid. Is this forbidden? Not at all; according to Islam, sex slaves are not at all forbidden. Quite the contrary, the rules regulating sex-slaves differ from those for free women [i.e., Muslim women]. The prophet of Islam, Muhammed, legitimized sex slavery. This prevents our youth from being involved in adultery. For example, in the Chechnyan war, of course there are female Russian captives. So go and buy those and sell them here in Kuwait; better that than for the men to engage in forbidden sexual relations[105]."

While it is correct to say that there are sincere, peace loving Muslims who apply Islam only to themselves, the ultimate goal of every true Muslim is to be like that true and ultimate Muslim, the Founder of Islam, Muhammed himself. He was the one who initiated the detailed directions for having slaves as part of Islam. There were leaders before him who lived and taught that slavery was wrong. If he had been genuinely looking for a model society, he could have learned from them. If, as he claims, he was receiving divine revelation for each directive in the Quran, any sincere person must ask which divinity was speaking to him. While sex slavery is a global issue, only in Islam does it get a religious stamp of approval. Every nation which has been attacked or invaded by Muslims experiences the process of the slaughter of its men, and the slavery of its women and children[106].

Abdiya Wesab

Glossary

This glossary does not include words from the Appendix because those words are clearly explained in context.

Word	Meaning, history or explanation
Abbot of Kostamonitou on Athos	The Kostamonitou is one of the monasteries atMt Athos
Abkhazia	Part of modern Georgia.
Akshamsaddin	Influential Ottoman religious scholar and advisor to Mehmed II.
al-Insān al-Kāmil	Translates as 'the only perfect man who exemplified to humans the morality of God.' Which is what Muslims believe of Muhammed.
Allah	God
Allah	The term for God in Arabic
Amasya	Called Amasia in antiquity, it was a Pontus city from 333BC to 26BCC. Under Rome it was a metropolis, passing then to Byzantine rule until 1075 when the Turks took it.
Amazon	A tribe of warrior women who lived in Asia Minor.
Anatolia	Also known as Asia Minor, it is the westernmost part of Asia, and now makes up the bulk of modern Turkey.
Anna Hâtûn	Daughter of David of Trebizond, who was married by force to Zaganos, who divorced her when she would not convert to Islam.
Apostle	A Greek term that was given to people who were sent on mission under authority as envoy or delegate.

Mara Hâtûn

Word	Meaning, history or explanation
Aq-Quyunlu tribe	The White Sheep Tribe of Turkomans was a Persian, Sunni Turkish federation of tribes which held parts of eastern Anatolia from 1378-1501. They also ruled parts of Armenia, Azerbaijan, Iran and Iraq.
Avalona	A now historical place in the Ceraunian Mountains, running down to the Shkumbin River in Albania.
Ayas Pasha	A vizier
Ayna	There were many women available to the Sultan as concubines. These are never named, historically, unless they give birth to a child which the Sultan decides to recognize as his own. Ayna would be an example of one of these women .
Aynışah, Hundi, and Sultanzade	three of Bayezid's daughters
Bayezid's wives	p.452-453 - because there are many, I refer you to the pages where their details are.
Bayramiye Sufi Order in Constantinople	A Sufi order is like a denomination within Islam. Sufis (explained under that heading) had lodges or tekkes, where masters taught disciples. Akshemeddin founded this order because Bayram-Veli had been his master.
ben	Means son of in Hebrew.
Beška	Village in Serbia
Bey	Lord
Beyazid II	Son of Mehmed II, he was Sultan from1481-1512.
Beylerbey	literally 'Lord of Lords', a Beylerbey is an Ottoman ruler who rules over other Beys.
binti-Abdullah	When people were converted to Islam - by choice or by slavery - they were given the new last name binti-Abdullah. Binti is a term that indicates sonship or descendants.
Bosnia	Initially Illyrian, it eventually became Serbia and Croatian until the Ottoman conquest in 1463.
Boza	Fermented millet beverage, served warm, with cinnamon. It may have begun in the Balkans but spread across the Ottoman Empire. Some sources say that it was also popular in ancient Sumarian tribes as arsikku and ar-zig.

Abdiya Wesab

Word	Meaning, history or explanation
Brankovići	One of four royal families lines which gave Emperors to the Byzantine throne and rulers to other Balkan domains before Ottoman conquest.
Bulgaria	Home to the Karanovo culture in 6,500 BC, over time Thracians, Phrygians, Persians and Celts all had influence here. Under Rome it was united with the region. Eventually the Bulgar Turks conquered in the late 7th century.
Bursa	Historical cities have been here since 5200BC. The Greeks built the city of Prusa here in 202BC. Bursa became the capitol of the Ottoman Empire in 1326AD.
bürümcük	Crepe overskirt and bodice with sleeves
byrek	A dish made with fillo dough. If made savory, it is usually filled with feta cheese and green vegetables. Sometimes it is made with ground or cubed beef, pine nuts and onions. If it is sweet, the dish becomes a form of baklava.
Byzantium	The city at the center of the Byzantine Empire which later was called Constantinople.
Çandarlı Halil Pasha	Grand vizier to both Sultan's Murad and his son Mehmed II
çaşnigirs	Tasters of food and drink for the sultan.
Cem	Was the third son of Sultan Memhed II, who fought his brother for the throne. Eventually he went to Europe and was kept there are a political prisoner.
Ceraunian Mountains	Location of Scutari - Shkodra
Cevbiri	Belt women wore which hooked in front.
Challah	Bread made by Jewish people, often used for Sabath
Charoset	A dish made with apples and walnuts, honey and cinnamon. It is always served at Passover to commemorate the material used to make bricks in Egypt, but it tastes amazing!
Chemise	A woman's loose, shirt-like undergarment
Church of St. George	built by Đurađ II Balšić on Beška Island, in Lake Skadar. He was Aunt Jelena's husband.

Ɗara Ɦâꞇûn

Word	Meaning, history or explanation
Çiçek Hâtûn	One of the wives of Mehmed II, mother of Cem, who fought with Bayezid for the throne.
cilt	Book binding
coenobitic	Monks who focus outward on their local communities.
Constantine	The first Emperor of the Byzantine Empire who established Constantinople in 330AD, building it upon the ruins of Byzantium.
Constantine XI Palaiologos	The last Byzantine Emperor of Constantinople.He ruled from 1449 to 1453, dying in the conquest of Constantinople.
Constantinople	The city which is now called Istanbul.
Coptic	The Copts are indigenous to North and Eastern Africa. Coptic Christians are the largest denomination in the region.
Costanzo da Ferrara	a painter and medalist from Naples who went to Constantinople to paint a portrait of the Sultan Mehmed II between 1475–1478. He remained at the court until the Sultan's death and produced a commemorative medal of him.
Costanzo da Ferrara	Medalist who created a commemorative medal of Mehmed
Count Vlad of Wallachia	Vlad was taken as a child in the Ottoman tithe of boys. His father and brother were murdered. Vlad retuned to his homeland as an Ottoman soldier, and wanted to rule, but when he didnt' succeed took retribution by impaling people. Because he massacred so many people he became known as Dracula. More correctly, his father's house was called Drăculești, which became synonymous with being bloodthirsty.
Crimean Khanate	Was a Turkish state from 1441 to 1783 started by Toqa Temur, one of the grandsons of Genghis Khan.
Crimean Tatars	A Turkish ethnic group who live in Crimea. They moved into the region around the 10th century.
Cuma	Friday, the Muslim day of prayer

Abdiya Wesab

Word	Meaning, history or explanation
Damat	Bridegroom or son-in-law
Dardanelles	Also called the Hellespontes historically, this strait between Europe and Asia is at the furthest point west in Northwestern Turkey.
Dârü's-saâde-i Sinop	The Palace of Sinop
Deftardar	Ottoman minister of finances.
Despot	Lord or Master was a senior title for sons or sons-in-law of members of the Byzantine royal family. Eventually the term was used in Bulgarian and Serbian. The regions that these people ruled were called despotates, as in the Despotate of Epirius, Morea and Serbia.
devşirme system	The system created by the Sultan to have on in five sons of Jews and Christians tithed to the Sultan. These boys were enslaved, and trained to either serve as page boys, eunuchs, or frontline soldiers.
Dhimmi	A term for non-Muslims living in an Islamic state with 'protection' which they buy with a special, high tax called Jizya.
Didymóteichon in Evros	A town on the eastern edge of Evros in northeastern Greece
Divan Road	"Road to the Imperial Council" in Constantinople, built upon the same route that Constantine built the Mese, or main boulevard leading from the Seraglio point to the main gate in the city walls which led on down the Via Egnatia, or road to Rome. Constantine had mile markers which stared at the Milion, a tower the head of this road.
Doğmamış çocuğa don biçilmez.	"Don't cut cloth out for a child that has not been born yet"
Dubočica and Toplica	Part of the land which came to the Sultan as part of Mara's dowry
Dulkadirid	A beylik kingdom which reached from Kirsehir to Mosul and was a buffer state between the Ottomans and Mamluk Sultanate. Several Dulkadirid princesses became political wives of Sultans to maintain the relationship.
Đurađ	A male name meaning George.

Ɗara Ꮝâᴄûn

Word	Meaning, history or explanation
Đurađ Branković	was the Serbian leaders from 1427-1456. He was the last true Serbian ruler. After his rule, the Serbians were vassals to the Ottomans.
Ebru	Oil painting on paper or cloth made by putting oil on water, creating a design, and then laying the paper or cloth on top of it
Edirne	Historically Uskudama in the BC era, with Emperor Hadrain rebuilding it as Adrianopolis. In 1369 the Ottomans built their fourth capitol city here.
Eid al-Fitr	Holiday to celebrate the end of Ramadan
Éla! Éla	come, come now, come around, come what may
Elbistan	A city currently in the Kahramanmaras province, the city belonged the Dulkadir before the Ottomans. It is close to Harran which is where Abraham and his family lived before he moved east, following God.
Elisabeth, Herman and Georg	The children of Katarina and Ulrich Ceilo. Elizabeth married Matthias Corvinus in an attempt to unite Hungary, but she died with the year.
Emine Gülbahar Hâtûn	Also known as Mükrime, she was one of the wives of Mehmed II. She was a "binti-Abdullah", or woman taken in slavery who was told that she was Muslim. Her real name was Justine and she came from Albania.
Emine Hâtûn	Was the principle consort of Sultan Mehmed I. She was of the Dulkadirid Tribe, and the mother of Murad II, who became Sultan.
Epiphany	Is a season in the Christian calendar which celebrates that God chose to reveal Himself to mankind incarnate as Jesus Christ. The word also means revelation.
Ertine Hâtûn	Was daughter of Şadgeldi Paşazade Mustafa Bey of the Kutluşah of Amasya. She was also known as Yeni Hâtûn, or the new wife. She had two daughters.
Erusaghēmi Patriark'ut'iwn	the Patriarch of the Armenian church in Jerusalem.
Euboea	A large Greek island, second only to Crete
eunuch	A male who has been emasculated.
Euphrates River	One of two rivers which ran across historical Mesopotamia, and now run in eastern Turkey.

Abdiya Wesab

Word	Meaning, history or explanation
Euxine Sea	Black Sea
Eyüp Camii	A mosque built on the estimated site of the grave of Eyüp Ensari, in Constantinople, which also happened to be the site of the Anargyroi or Kosmidion monastery, founded in the 5th century. The area was considered a holy site to Muslims after the mosque was built and foreigners could not come there.
Eyüp Ensari	Standard-bearer for the Prophet Mohammed, who is said to have died in the first attack upon Constantinople. Akshemeddin, Mehmed II's religious advisor, is said to have discovered his grave upon the conquest of the city.
Ezeba and Doxompus, in the valley of the river Strymon.	The region where Mehmed II bequeathed Mara with a homer her diplomatic services to his throne.
Ezogelin Çorba	A type of lentil soup which has other veggies in it with spices.
Fatih	Conqueror
Fatih Camii	"The Conqueror's Mosque" built by Mehmed II on the site of the Church of the Apostles, where the early church fathers had been venerated.
Ferace	Outer garment worn by women in the Sultan's harem
fitna	Rebellion or social disturbance, which is considered worse than murder.
fitra	original state' as per Islamic belief, that Allah restores people to an original sinless state when they the 'revert' to Islam.
Friar Bartholomew of Epirus	A loyal supporter of Skenderbeg.
Gavur	infidel
Gazi	Is a title of honor given to men who participate in *ghazw*, or military expeditions or raids modeled on the conquest raids led by the Islamic leader and prophet Muhammed.
geç olsun güç olmasın,	better late than more difficult later

Word	Meaning, history or explanation
Gedik Ahmed Pasha	Vizier and beylerbey and Kapudan or Grand Admiral of the Sultan's armies.
Genoa	Genoa was a Republic starting in 1005. The Genoese remained autonomous until 1797. It always had a large fleet, and also had port cities which it owned as trading station in Crimea.
Georgia	Is a nation in the Caucasus at the crossroads of Western Asia and Eastern Europe.
Geraniums and camomile, anchusa and acanthus, ebenus and phlomis	Flowers that grow from cutting which are found in Greece
Göde Ahmed	Grandson of Mehmed II and Justine, son of Gevherhan and Ugurlu Muhammed.
gökçe munçu	Blue glass amulet common in many Turkic tribes, now called nazar boncuk, nazar being the Arabic word for surveillance. It is believed to protect from what is termed the evil eye. The evil eye is a power to cast a spell upon someone just by looking askance at them.
Göksu and Küçüksü	These are two streams which run into the Bosphorus which are fed from the Mountain of Alem.
Gözde	Someone who is always in view
Grgur Branković	Son of Đurađ Branković and brother of Mara. He was blinded by the Sultan.
Gülşah	one of the wives of Mehmed II, mother of Mustafa
Gülşirin Hâtûn, Oğuzhan, Murad, Gevhermülük, and Ayşe.	The wife and children of Cem, son of Sultan Mehmed II
Haci	A haci or hadji is a man who has taken his pilgrimage to Mecca, which is one of the five pillars of faith required of each Muslim.
Haci-Bayrami-Veli	Was a Muslims poet and founder of the Bayrami Sufi order.

Abdiya Wesab

Word	Meaning, history or explanation
Haghia	Saint
Haghia Sophia	"Church of Holy Wisdom" built in 537AD by Justiniain Constantinople.
Halal	An Arabic word which means permissible or lawful. It is the opposite of *haram*, which is forbidden and unlawful.
Haliç	Turkish name for the Golden Horn, because could look like a scimitar, which is the meaning of Haliç
Halime Hâtûn	Halime was Murad II's first wife and daughter of Isfendiyar Bey, ruler of the Isfendiyarids. Also sometimes called Sultan Hâtûn, she was the mother of Ahmed and Alaeddin, both of whom were killed under suspicious conditions. Her youngest son was called Küçük Ahmed, and is believed to have been secreted away to India, where he founded the Bijapur dynasty. Halime was forced to remarry when Murad died. She and her second husband, advisor to the Sultan, Ishak Pasha, had eight children.
han	Inn
Hanukkah	חֲנֻכָּה Hanukkah is the Jewish Festival which remembers the dedication of the Second Temple in Jerusalem at the time of the Maccabean Revolt. It is celebrated for eight nights and days starting on the 25th day of Kislev in the Hebrew calendar. The central feature of the festival is a Menorah candleholder. A candle is lit each night. These commemorate the rededication of the temple. The oil which is used in the temple is prepared in a special way, which takes a week to prepare. In the time of the Maccabees when the temple was reopened, they had only enough oil for one night. They decided to light that oil in faith, and the oil lasted the week while the other oil was been prepared.
Harem	The part of the house reserved for the female members of a household.
Hâtûn	The term use to be polite to someone who is the wife of an important person.
Herod	There were several Herods. Herod the Great lived from about 73BC to 4AD. Herod Antipas was the one who had John the Baptist murdered. Herod Agrippa I was the grandson of Herod the Great (Acts12) who persecuted the early church and murdered the apostle James.

Mara Hâtûn

Word	Meaning, history or explanation
Hilandar monastaries	Monasteries which are part of the Mt Athos family
hodja	Teacher and priest
hoşaf	A Turkish dessert made of dried fruits and seasoned with cinnamon.
Hüdavendigar	God's gift
Hüma Hâtûn	Was a slave taken in the capture of Thesoloniki. Typical of slaves taken to the Harem, she was binti-Abdullah, which meant that she was told that she was a "daughter of Abdullah", end of story. Slaves had no personal opinion, much less so if the were women.Hüma Hâtûn's real name was Stella, and it is likely that she was Jewish. She was the mother of Mehmed II and had several daughters.
Hunkâr Sofrasi	the great room, used only to host the Sultan.
iç entari	A shirt or loose robe
iç oğlan	one of the boys who were allowed into the inner palace and served the Sultan's chambers.
iddah	Mourning period assigned to those who have lost loved ones, especially relevant to widows whose relatives will often marry them off to another man at this point, especially if they are still young.
Iftar	Dusk meal served to break the day long fast of Ramadan
Ikbal	Woman who is fortunate, in this context, as being someone chosen by the Sultan
Imam	Priest
Imbros	Now called Gökçeada, is an island in the Aegean
Inegöl	A city in the province of Bursa
Infidel	Term used to accuse others of unbelief of those aspects of their religion which must be followed to stay loyal.
Ishak Pasha	was the Beylerbey, or "Lord of Lords" The man whom Halime Hâtûn had to marry when Sultan Murad II died.

Abdiya Wesab

Word	Meaning, history or explanation
Islands of Santa Maura, Kefalonia, and Zante.	Islands in tht Aegean
Ivan Crnojević	had been endowed with Zeta when Aunt Jelena's husband died. He had fought with Venice to help this neighboring land, risking his life on many occasions to defend the city by water and land.
Jacob, the Bishop of Smederovo	Bishop appointed to serve in the church which Mara's father built
Jandar Turkoman	This people group are also called the Isfendiyarids and had a dynasty which ruled from 1292-1461 in parts of Anatolia, which is now in modern Turkey. The region was called Paphlagonia in the Roman period. The Jandar Turkoman were annexed by Mehmed II in 1461.
Jannisary	New force of soldiers, *Yeniçeri, as it came to be called over time*
Jelisaveta	Wife of Grgur Branković.
Ježevo and Mravince	The location where Mara's home was, which she bequeathed to the monasteries, with the care of the local women who were widows from this area.
Jizya	Tax of people who are not Muslims in an Islamic State.
John Komnenos	One of the royal lines of Byzantium, of which Mehmed the Conqueror claimed lineage.
Julian of Norwich	British author and well known medieval anchorite of a monastery. She wrote 'Revelations of Divine Love' and was known in the churches.
kadayif-i hassa.	A ceremonial desert only ever served to the Mother of the Sultan and to the Sultan himself. No one else was allowed to eat this delicacy.
kadife	Velvet
Kadın	Literally means woman who is a wife, in the context of the Sultan it means one of the four wives the Sultan had at one time
Kaftan	A type of tunic

Word	Meaning, history or explanation
Kantakuzēnoi	One of four royal families lines which gave Emperors to the Byzantine throne and rulers to other Balkan domains before Ottoman conquest.
Kapalıçarşı	Covered built by Mehmed II with about 2,000 inside shops.
Kapudan	Grand Admiral of the Ottoman Navy
Karagöz and Hacivat	Puppets that entertain during Ramadan
Karamanids	One of the Anatolian Beyliks, which was the most powerful from the 1300s until 1487.
Karnakata	Is a district in India where Yusuf Adil became Sultan of Bijapur.
kaşbastı	diadem placed on the head of a Sultan's "wife", embellished with a stone which centers on her forehead. It indicates her rank in the Ottoman palace. It is placed upon her head like a seal, a type of final stamp to ratify the deal.
Kastamonu	Is a city and district north of Ankara, not far from the Black Sea.
Katarina	Youngest daughter of Ðuraď Branković, and sister of Mara.
Katherina Lola	Servant to Halime in our story, who secretly rescued Küçük Ahmed and was his surrogate mother in India.
Katmer	Layered flatbread
kemha	brocade
Keşkek	Pounded wheat with butter
Kiler Odasi	Office of the Pantry in the Topkapi Palace.
King Matthias Corvinus	King Matthias Corvinus, who had indicated that he would enabled Vuk to take the title Despot of Serbia.
Kirtle	A woman's dress or skirt
Kosovo	Now a partial recognized state ins Southeastern Europe.

473

Abdiya Wesab

Word	Meaning, history or explanation
Küçük Ahmed	It is not fully known if this son of Murad was killed by Mehmed II in fratricide, or if he escaped. Some historians believe that he became Yusuf Adil, who founded the Adil Shahi dynasty as Sultan of Bijapur in India. His dynasty continued for two centuries.
külliye	Compound around a mosque
Kutlushah	Celebrated Leader, a term which means Congratulations in modern Turkmeni.
kuyu kebab	Meat that has been prepared in an old, abandoned well
Ladislas	Called Ladislas the Magnanimous, he was the King of Naples during the reign of Sultan Murad.
Lanier	Vendor of wool
Latin Church	The church in Europe which was not Orthodox, sometimes also called Catholic, which is a misnomer, because the term catholic means united.
law of fratricide	Taking the concept of killing ones brothers and making it law.
Lazar Branković	Youngest brother of Mara and son of Đurađ Branković.
Leon Makelos monastery	Monastery where each Emperor and ruler had been consecrated during the Byzantine Empire, near the city walls of Constantinople. Now the site of the Eyup Mosque and considered shrine of Islam that non-Muslims may not go to .
Lezha, Drisht and Žablijak Crnojevića	Towns near Shkodër, Albania
lokanta	Restaurant, usually a mom and pop place, local to a neighborhood
lokum	Turkish Delight
Lygos	LYgos was the initial settlement which was later called Byzantium. It was begun in 7BC by the Phrygians.
mahalle	Neighborhoods
Mahmud Pasha Angelović	One of Sultan Mehmed II's viziers.

Mara Ḣâtûn

Word	Meaning, history or explanation
Makr	To deceive, delude, double-cross, be cunning, sly, willy. https://www.answering-islam.org/authors/cornelius/makr.html
Manisa	Historically a Phrygian and then Lydian city in the Aegean region of Asia Minor, about 62km from the biblical city of Sardis. In the Roman era it was called Magnesia ad Sipylum. In 1076 the Selcuks Muslims took the city. It was returned to Byzantine rule for a brief period, but taken again by the Ottomans.
Mara Hâtûn	Daughter of Đurađ Branković, Mara was a political bride of the Sultan and the fourth wife. She did not have children, and it is likely that the marriage was not consummated.
Maria Gattilusio	The widow of Alexander, brother of David of Trebizond.
Marmara Sea	Historically called the Propontis, this inland sea connects the Aegean and Black Seas. It is thought that at one point it was complete landlocked, and that the Bosphorus and other rivers that currently feed it were but streams.
Maslaha	Quranic term of placing the public's interest above any personal interest must be applied to decide an issue
Matbah-i Âmire Emânet	The Office of Imperial Kitchen in the Topkapi palace.
meddah	Storyteller
medrese	Muslim school
Mehd-i-ulya	Cradle of the Great, the title given to the Mother of the Sultan in the early 1400s
Mehmed II	Also called Mehmed the Conqueror, ruled as Ottoman Sultan from 1444-1446, then again from 1451-1481. He conquered Constantinople.
Mercimek Çorba	A smooth lentil soup which is creamy.
Michael Kritobulus of Imbros	Michael was a landowner on this formerly Genoese island near the shores of Asia Minor. He had led the citizens to peaceably approach the Sultan to live harmoniously within the Ottoman Empire. He was respected by the Sultan for this, and might gain audience with him easily. Michael was also an author, and was given to pay great detail to history. He wrote a bio of Mehmed

Abdiya Wesab

Word	Meaning, history or explanation
millet	a religious and ethnic group of people with a religion other than Islam.
Milliner	A person who designs, makes, trims or sells hats.
Molla Gürani	One of the tutors that Mehmed II was raised by, along with Akshamsaddin and Zaganos.
moré	A drink made of mulberries
Moses ben Elijah Capsali	Born in Venetian held Crete in 1420, he studied in German before moving to Constaninople, where he became a rabbi during the reign of Sultan Mehmed. He was given the title of Hakkim Bashi - or chief judge - for his services as a good judge.
Mount Athos	An island region in Greece where a series of monasteries have been built for the last 2,000 years.
muhallebi	Milky pudding
mukarrrib	Arabic term for 'priest-kings' or federators.
Murad I	Ottoman Sultan from 1362 to 1389, proceeded by Orhan, succeeded by Bayezid I.
Murad II	Ottoman Sultan from 1421 to 1444, and again from 1446 to 1451. Predecessor: Mehmed I, successor: Mehmed II.
Muraqqa	An album of miniature paintings
Mustafa	Son of Mehmed II and Gülşah Hatun, he was poisoned upon suspicious of adultery with the wife of one of the Viziers.
Mustafa Kemal Atatürk	The name of the man who helped the Ottoman Empire transition into modern Turkey.
Mutancana	Rich lamb, slow-cooked with apricots, figs, grapes, and almonds
nahile	Districts of a town

Word	Meaning, history or explanation
Nakkashane-i-Rum	An art form which was developed to illuminate literature, provide calligraphy, marbling, and book binding. When something ends with the term *"i-Rum"* it means that it entered the culture from the Greeks or Romans. The *Nakkashane* was formed in Constantinople in the void left by the destruction of the Scriptoriums. The art of the Persians and Italians were researched and merged into this new type of Scriptorium which sprung up in the late 1400s.
Nargile	A method of smoking in which the smoke is drawn through a water pipe.
Nehemiah	A biblical hero and leaders who led the people to rebuild the city of Jerusalem upon the command of the King of Persia.
Nemanjići	One of four royal families lines which gave Emperors to the Byzantine throne and rulers to other Balkan domains before Ottoman conquest.
Nergis	Daffodil
Nergiszade	Granddaughter of Mehmed II, and daughter of Mustafa.
Nicea	Historical site of the first and second counsels of the early church. This city is now called Iznik.
Nicholas Moneta	was related to Mara through Aunt Olivera were also present. Nicolas had sent his wife and five children to Venice ahead of the war, when Shkodra came under siege.
Notos wind	Southerly wind in Aegean
Olivera	Also known as Despina Hâtûn, she was a political wife to sultan Bayezid I, and aunt to Mara Hâtûn.
opus Dei	Is Latin for the work of God. It is the term given to the communal prayers, which met eight times around the clock for liturgy, based on the Psalms.

Word	Meaning, history or explanation
Orthodox Church	The Orthodox Church in the context of this book focuses on the Eastern Orthodox. The term orthodox means to conform to established doctrine. Greek is the most prevalent language spoken by those who are part of the Orthodox Church. The Orthodox and Latin or Catholic churches had a schism for a time, which has now been unified.
Orthódoxo Ellinikó Patriarcheío Ierosolýmon	the Orthodox Greek Patriarchate of Jerusalem
Osman *Gazi*	Also called Osman I was the leaders of the Ottoman Turks and founder of the Ottoman Dynasty.
Otranto	Otranto was originally an Illyrian town called Hydrus which was upgraded to a city under the Romans. The city was Byzantine and then came under the leadership of the Norman Robert Guiscard. The city was multinational and home to a school started by the Jews.
Paidi mou	My child
Palaiologoi	One of four royal families lines which gave Emperors to the Byzantine throne and rulers to other Balkan domains before Ottoman conquest.
Pastelicos	**Spinach feta pastries, often called börek or byrek in the Balkans and Turkey**
patitiri	Wine press commonly used in Greece.
Patriarch Gennadius	He was the Patriarch of Constantinople under Mehmed II, and led from 1454-1464. He was asked to, and wrote an exposition of his faith for Mehmed II, called 'Confession'.
pederasty	The sexual abuse of boys at the hands of men
pelamide	A type of fish
Peloponnesian Peninsula	A peninsula in southern Greece, connected by the isthmus of Corinth.
Pera	Meaning 'beyond' in Greek, was a part of Constantinople which was outside the city walls, on the other side of the Golden Horn. It became the part of the city that diplomats and foreigners were assigned to and is now essentially city center for Istanbul.

Word	Meaning, history or explanation
Pharisee	The Pharisees were a religious order in Judaism who founded rabbinic Judaism. They were legalistic and increased the number of biblical laws, almost doubling them, in order to keep people from sinning. Most of their new laws were against women.
Pişmaniye	Candy which looks like spun silk
Princess Gevherhan Hâtûn	Daughter of Gülbahar Hâtûn and MehmedII, sister of future Sultan Bayezid.
Prophet Mohammed	The man whom Muslims follow. He initiated Islam, after spending time in the wilderness alone where he reported having being visited by Gabriel and getting revelation from Allah. He taught that submission to Allah was the only right life and religion, and that he was the last prophet sent by Allah. He taught that revelation was abrogated, meaning that if a later revelation contrasted with an earlier one, the later revelation ruled out the earlier one. In this way, he, as the last prophet, abrogated anything that any earlier prophet may have said that contradicted with him. And any revelation that Muhammed himself receive earlier in life was abrogated by later revelations.
protovestiarios	A high court position in the Byzantine courts.
Qanun	The world for law in Arabic.
Qayser-i-Rûm	Roman Caesar
Quran	The holy book of the Muslims
raison d'être	Reason to exist
Ramadan	A month of fasting employed by Muslims who fast from sunup to sundown.
Rhodes	the largest Dodecanese island of the Greek islands in the Aegean.
Roman Empire	The Empire started by Rome, which began in 27BC and continued until 1453.The Siege of Constantinople technically ended the last vestiges of the Roman Empire, but Sultan Mehmed called himself the Kayser-i-Rum, claiming his authority over that legacy.

Abdiya Wesab

Word	Meaning, history or explanation
Rome	Capitol city of the Roman Empire
Rûmeli Hisar	The castle built on the European side of the Bosphorus at the behest of Mehmed II with which he staved off travel in the Bosphorus as part of his strategy of taking Constantinople.
Rûmelia	Etymologically 'land of the Romans', under the Ottomans it came to be a term applied to the Balkans.
Sahlep	Orchid root drink
Salat	Prayer times
Salonika or Salonica	Modern day Thessaloniki
şalvar	Baggy trousers worn by women
Sanjakbey	A Sanjakbey was a 'Lord of the Standard' answerable only to the Turban of the Sultan himself.
Santa Maura, Kefalonia, and Zante	Islands in the Aegean
Saruca	Saruca was one of Murad's counselors
Saruhan	One of the Ottoman Beyliks near Manisa, also called the Sarukhanids
Saz	Long handled string instrument
Schezade or Şehezade or Şehzade	Princess
Scriptorium	Literally a place for writing in Latin. These were rooms which were common in medieval monasteries and the homes of people who were educated for the writing, copying, and illuminating of manuscripts, especially the Bible.

ᴔara Ꮒâᴛûn

Word	Meaning, history or explanation
Scutari	Refers to several places. The town of Shkodër, Albania was known as Scutrai in Italian and when it became an Ottoman province it was called the Sanjak of Scutari. Interestingly, the town of Üsküdar, in Istanbul was formerly known as Scutari as well. This may be beacuse Toman gladiators used the Italli sputum shields which were called Scutari in clasification.
Selamlik	The part of the house which is reserved for male members of a household.
Selymbria	A town of Thrace founded by Byzas, who also founded Byzantium. Under Rome the name was changed to Eudoxiupolis. It was named Silivri after the Ottoman conquest.
Seraglio	A large harem in the sultan's palace
Seraser	Velvet with metallic threads
Serbia	Serbia has been on the map from the Stone Age, but it's borders have varied depending on its era.
Shamash	שׁמָשׁ The term given to the candle in the middle of the Menorah candelabrum which has nine branches. Shamash means servant. This central candle serves or attends the other candles because it is the one used to light all the other candles, one each night. Another term for the Shamash is "Light of the World".
Shari'a	Islamic law which forms the basis for Islamic societies.
Sheikh	Islamic ruler, patriarch of an Islamic family, and a term of respect.
Shift	Loosely fitting dress that hangs straight.
Shkodra	Shkodër, Albania
Sigismund	Was king of Hungary and Croatia from 1387, but he was also considered to the the Holy Roman Emperor and ruled from Brandenburg. His kingdom grew to include Germany, Bohemia and Italy until 1437.
sipahi	Professional calvarymen trained and stationed by the Turkish rulers.
şiş kebab	Meat cooked on a skewer

Abdiya Wesab

Word	Meaning, history or explanation
Sittişah Hâtûn	Originally named Mükrime, she was the daughter of Süleyman Zülkadiroğlu Bey, and Mehmed II's first wife.
Sivas	Sebaste in Greek, it was a Roman Megalopolis prior to that. It was part of Armeniia during the Byzantine period, but was plundered by the Turkish 1059.
Skenderbeg	Gjergj Kastrioti was an Albanian nobleman's son taken as hostage to the Sultan's courts. He served the Sultan 20 years and then was able to return to his homeland where he gathered theAlbanian tribes and tried to lead them to defend the nation against the Ottomans. He led them for 25 years, and galvanized them as a people.
skete or *eremitic*	Monks who feel called to live as hermits, dedicated to fasting and praying.
Slavonic	The first slavic literary language
Smederevo	Built on the Danube, by Đurađ Branković with the Sultan's permission.
Spahis	Military leaders
Stamboul	Istanbul
Stefan Branković	Son of Đurađ Branković and brother of Mara. He was blinded by the Sultan.
Sublime Porte	Term used to describe the central government of the Ottoman Empire.
Sufism	Sufism was a popular form of Islam which dovetailed well with both the Janissaries and the intellectual mindset which was flourishing in court. It was believed that the man who sincerely followed the *Qanun* or laws of Allah in society, as laid out in the *Quran*, would be pleasing God by restoring themselves to their 'original state' or *fitra*. Muslims believed that people were born with the natural state of purity and innocence and they could revert to it by choice. Believing that people are naturally compassionate, intelligent, and of perfect excellence, the Sufi taught that people who became Muslims were reverting, not converting to Islam. They taught that Islam was the original religion and that Muhammed was God's last prophet.
Suhur	Pre-fast dawn meal during Ramadan
Süleyman Zülkadiroğlu Bey	6th Ruler of the Dulkadirs
talisman	An object that a person believes holds magic power.

Mara Hâtûn

Word	Meaning, history or explanation
Tamerlane	Also known as Timur, he was a conqueror in Asia who murdered millions of people who would not become Muslims.
taswir	Miniature painting
teşhir	a method of public shaming, which included being led through the streets with a cord through one's nose, smeared with soot, or placed backwards on an ass. Although itself shaming, teşhir was a way to heap added public shame on the one being led to punishment.
thawab	Spiritual rewards
Theodore Spandounis	His mother was of the Cantacuzenus family, his father, Matthew Spandounis entrusted Mara to train him. He went on to become a historian.
Thrace	The geographical region of southeastern Europe, which is now split between the Bulgarians Greeks and Turks. The Balkans border it to the north, the Black Sea to the east and the Aegean to the west.
Ti ginete!	How becoming!
Tolodoth	תּוֹלְדֹת in Hebrew means descendants.
Topkapi Saray	The Cannon Palace which Mehmed II built for himself and his family on the grounds of what had been ancient Byzantium.
Trebizond	Initially founded in 756BC as a Milesian trading colony on the Black Sea, it became a Byzantine State which flourished until the Ottoman conquest. It is now called Trabzon.
Uğurlu Muhammad	Son of Uzun Hasan, of the Aq-Quyunlu tribe, who switched allegiance to the Sultan.
ülema	Means the learned ones. Singularly, Alim is scholar. These are the guardians and interpreters of knowledge of Islamic doctrine and law. The Alim are educated in Madrassa.
Ulrich II of Celje	He was the captin general and regent of Hungary, and Lord of parts of Slovenia, Croatia, Bosnia, Austria, Serbia and Slovakia. He was husband of Katarina, who was sister of Mara, both daughters of Đurađ Branković.

483

Abdiya Wesab

Word	Meaning, history or explanation
Uludağ	The mountain near Bursa, which used to be called Mount Olympus in historical Asia Minor.
ustad	Master of a Trade
Uzun Hassan	Leader of the Aq Qoyunlu tribe. His son Uğurlu Muhammad went to Mehemed II and promised allegiance to him in war against his own father. Mehmed gave him his own daughter in marriage.
Valide Sultan	Means mother of the Sultan. The first title was *mehd-i ulya* or "cradle of the great", and later became Valide, or mother of the Sultan. This role was held by the legal mother of the person who was Sultan.
Varaždin Apostol'	A handwritten book of Orthodox liturgy written in 1454. It was named for the city of Varaždin, where it was written out.
vardar	A river in Macedonia, Albania and Greece, also a term for a north-eastern wind.
Via Egnatia	A road constructed by Romans in 2AD which ran through Illyricum, Thrace, Macedonia and connected to the Via Appia, which was the main route from Rome to Brindisi.
Vinum mustum	Is young wine, which contains the skins, seeds ans teams of the fruit. The solids are called a pomace and together are the first steps in wine making.
Vizier	Advisor to the Sultan
Vuk Grgurević Branković	Son of Grgur and Jelisavita, who became the titular Despot of Serbia from 1471 to 1485. He is honored in Serbian epic poetry for valor and heroism. He also founded the Gregeteg monastery.
Wallachia	Is a historical region of current Romania.
wives of Bayezid	on pages 436-7
Yeñiçeri or Janissaries	Literally the "new force" which was a frontline military unit formed by the Sultans from the tithe of Christian boys.
Yorgan	Quilt
Yorganji	Man who sells quilts

ᴅara ᕼâᴛûn

Word	Meaning, history or explanation
Yusuf	The Turkish name for Joseph
Zaganos	Zaganos was an Albanian boy taken in *devşirme*, who became a tutor to Mehmed. He advanced to the post of Vizier to Mehmed.

Bibliography

Whenever reference is not giving for which translation or version of the Bible is used, I have used The Berean Bible (www.Berean.Bible) Berean Study Bible (BSB) © 2016-2020 by Bible Hub and Berean.Bible.

[1] https://istanbul.com/blog/istanbul-travel-quotes/

[2] Musnad Ahmad, Al Hakim, al Jami' al Saghir and "Islam: From the Prophet Muhammad to the Capture of Constantinople Volume 2: Religion and Society" by Bernard Lewis

[3] Evliya Çelebi in "Seyahatname"

[4] https://www.britannica.com/event/Fall-of-Constantinople-1453 Shepard, J. The Cambridge History of the Byzantine Empire c.500-1492. Cambridge University Press, 2009.

[5] 'The Companion Guide to Istanbul and Around the Marmara' By John Freely, Anthony Glyn p.31

[6] Frantzes, Georgios; Melisseidis (Melisseides), Ioannis (Ioannes) A.; Zavolea-Melissidi, Pulcheria (2004). Εάλω η Πόλις·το χρονικό της άλωσης της Κωνσταντινούπολης: Συνοπτική ιστορία των γεγονότων στην Κωνσταντινούπολη κατά την περίοδο 1440 – 1453 [*The City has Fallen: Chronicle of the Fall of Constantinople: Concise History of Events in Constantinople in the Period 1440–1453*] (in Greek) (5 ed.). Athens: Vergina Asimakopouli Bros. ISBN 9607171918.

[7] T.S. Eliot (September 26, 1888–January 4, 1965) *Burnt Norton*, the first of his epic *Four Quartets*

[8] İnalcık, Halil (1997). "Istanbul". In van Donzel, E.; Lewis, B.; Phellat, Ch. (eds.). *Encyclopaedia of Islam*. 4 (2nd ed.). Leiden: Brill. pp. 224–248. ISBN 9789004057456

[9] Sakaoğlu, Necdet (1993–94). "İstanbul'un adları" [The names of Istanbul]. *Dünden bugüne İstanbul ansiklopedisi* (in Turkish). Istanbul: Türkiye Kültür Bakanlığı.

Abdiya Wesab

10 Robinson, Richard D. (1965). The First Turkish Republic: A Case Study in National Development. Cambridge: Cambridge University Press

11 George Sphrantzes. *The Fall of the Byzantine Empire: A Chronicle by George Sphrantzes 1401–1477*. Translated by Marios Philippides. University of Massachusetts Press, 1980. ISBN 978-0-87023-290-9.

12 Masters, Bruce (2009). "Millet". In Ágoston, Gábor; Bruce Masters (eds.). *Encyclopedia of the Ottoman Empire*. pp. 383–4.

13 Head, Constance (1977), "+Manuel and Helena" Imperial Twilight: The Palaiologos Dynasty and the Decline of Byzantium, Nelson-Hall, p. 145,

14 Bryer, Anthony (1975). "Greeks and Turkmens: The Pontic Exception" . *Dumbarton Oaks Papers*. Dumbarton Oaks. **29**: 113–148

15 Genesis 1:1

16 A Toladoth תּוֹלְדֹת is Hebrew for "generations" or "descendants" In the Genesis account, each time there is a transition between the teller, there is a new Toladoth. See Genesis 2:4 for the generations of the earth, 5:1 for Adam, 10:1 for Noah etc. It is believed that God wrote the first Toladoth, gave the book to Adam, who wrote his Toladoth, and passed it on.

17 Pliny the Elder, book IV, chapter XI:
"*On leaving the Dardanelles we come to the Bay of Casthenes, ... and the promontory of the Golden Horn, on which is the town of Byzantium, a free state, formerly called Lygos; it is 711 miles from Durazzo, ...*"

18 Boardman, John, ed. (1982). *The Cambridge Ancient History*. 10: Persia, Greece, and the Western Mediterranean. Cambridge, UK: Cambridge University Press. pp. 239–243. ISBN 978-0521228046.

19 Asutay-Effenberger, Neslihan (2007), Die Landmauer von Konstantinopel-Istanbul: Historisch-topographische und baugeschichtliche Untersuchungen, Walter de Gruyter, ISBN 978-3-11-019645-0p.2

20 J.J. Saunders, The history of the Mongol conquests p. 174, Routledge & Kegan Paul Ltd., 1971, ISBN 0812217667

21 https://www.answering-islam.org/Silas/childbrides.htm

22 'Oy u lisi' Lyrics and music author: народні; traditional Slavic folksong

23 Jeremiah 1:1-10 King James Bible

24 When the Jews experienced the Passover, they anointed the doorposts and lintels of their homes with the blood of the lamb which was slain, as the Lord had told them to. (Exodus 12) As God told them, the angel of death passed over them and they were protected. Jews eventually developed a mezuzah, which they hang on their door frame.In this little container are several Scriptures. They touch this coming and going to remind themselves of the Unity of God (Mishneh Torah, Laws of Mezuzah 6:13) and they kiss the finger that touched the Mezuzah to transfer the holiness to themselves. (Kitvei Arizal, vol. 12, Taamei Hamitzvot, Vaetchanan. See Rabbi Chaim Joseph David Azulai (1724–1806), known as the Chida, in his commentary Birkei Yosef to Shulchan Aruch, Yoreh De'ah 285:4.) Christians anoint their homes to remind themselves that when Jesus died on the Cross He was the Lamb of God that takes away the sins of the world. (John 1:29, Isaiah 53)

[25] Ali ibn Abu Taleb, founder of the Shiite sect of Islam said, "Alighty God created sexual desire in ten parts; then he gave nine parts to women and one to men." Geraldine Brooks, "Nine Parts of Desire", 1995

[26] Davis, Fanny (1986). "The Valide; The Ottoman Lady: A Social History from 1718 to 1918." ISBN 0-313-24811-7.

[27] 'Dzied' pa priekšu, brāļa māsa' a folksong of the Balkans

[28] Matthew 7:14

[29] Clement of Alexandria, "The Tutor" from "The Early Christians in their Own Words" edited by Eberhard Arnold, p.227

[30] Bukhari (Book #52, Hadith #220)

[31] Joseph von Hammer: *Osmanlı Tarihi* Vol I (condensation: Abdülkadir Karahan), Milliyet yayınları, İstanbul. pp 79-80 and Dimitris J. Kastritsis, The Sons of Bayezid: Empire Building and Representation in the Ottoman. Civil War of 1402-1413, Brill, 2007, ISBN 978-90-04-15836-8., xi.

[32] http://www.allaboutturkey.com/murat1.htm

[33] "Attargah", Old Turkic War Song, interpreted by folk band Altai Kai from Altai Republic

[34] "Nations of the Living, Nations of the Dead" by Mort Castle p. 161

[35] 'Jure, ustavai rana' (белорусская народная песня), Central European folk song, sung at harvest.

[36] Kermeli, Eugenia (2009). "Osman I". In Ágoston, Gábor; Bruce Masters (eds.). *Encyclopedia of the Ottoman Empire*. p. 445. Quoting: "Apart from these chronicles, there are later sources that begin to establish Osman as a mythic figure. From the 16th century onward a number of dynastic myths are used, endowing the founder of the dynasty with more exalted origins. Among these is recounted the famous "dream of Osman" which is supposed to have taken place while he was a guest in the house of a sheikh, Edebali. This is an example of eschatological mythology required by the subsequent success of the Ottoman emirate to surround the founder of the dynasty with supernatural vision, providential success, and an illustrious genealogy." And Imber, Colin (1987). "The Ottoman Dynastic Myth". *Turcica*. **19**: 7–27. "The attraction of Aşıkpaşazade's story was not only that it furnished an episode proving God had bestowed rulership on the Ottomans, but also it provided, with the physical descent from Oguz Khan, a spiritual descent. [...] Hence the physical union of Osman with a saint's daughter gave the dynasty a spiritual legitimacy and became, after the 1480s, an integral feature of dynastic mythology."

[37] Finkel, Caroline (2005). *Osman's Dream: The Story of the Ottoman Empire, 1300-1923*. Basic Books. p. 2., citing Lindner, Rudi P. (1983). *Nomads and Ottomans in Medieval Anatolia*. Bloomington: Indiana University Press. p. 37. ISBN 0-933070-12-8.

[38] A song by Mesihi, written in the 15th century, from "Flowers from a Persian Garden: And Other Papers" By William Alexander Clouston pp. 15-16

[39] Ephesians 2:6

[40] JPS Tanakh version of Psalm 57

[41] https://www.answering-islam.org/Women/in-hell.html

[42] "The Grand Turk" by John Freely

[43] Turkish rocking rhyme - "Fiś, fiś kayikji"

[44] part of the song by Lévon Minassian (Duduk) - " They Have Taken the One I Love " https://en.lyrics.co.kr/?p=622353

[45] John Freely (2009). The Grand Turk: Sultan Mehmet II - Conqueror of Constantinople, Master of an Empire and Lord of Two Seas. I.B.Tauris. ISBN 978-0-857-73022-0.

[46] Acts 17:27

[47] Mark 6:10, Genesis5:2a, Galatians 3:28a, Genesis 1:28

[48] J. V. A. Fine, "The Late Medieval Balkans, A Critical Survey from the Late Twelfth Century to the Ottoman Conquest" (1994), page 531

[49] Matthew 12:33

[50] "Creator of the Starry Night" Words: Conditor alme siderum, Ambrosian, 6th or 7th Century, trans. John Mason Neale, 1851 Source: W. H. Monk and C. Steggall, eds., *Hymns Ancient and Modern* (London, William Clowes and Sons, Old Edition, 1889), Hymn 45

[51] "Decline and Fall of Byzantium to the Ottoman Turks: An Annotated Translation of "Historia Turco-Byzantina" 1341-1462" Doukas p. 176

[52] Konstantin Jirecek, in *Geschicte der Serben*, vol 2 (Gotha 1918) p. 166 explains that the innermost walls of the fort were completed in 1430, but Mihalovic - a former Ottoman Janissary who was Serbian, and recorded history at this time - noted that the castle as a whole was still unfinished in 1439.

[53] '*The Holy Wars of King Wladislas and Sultan Murad*' by John Jefferson (2012) p.107

[54] A *defterdar* recorded every detail of what the Sultan owned and controlled. According to Inalcik in "Ottoman Methods" p. 125 and forward, this was a position of central authority.

[55] A '*mukarrib*' is a Kuranic teacher who expounded the Kuran in the presences of the Sultan during the month of Ramadan. Translation from Redhouse Press Ottoman Turkish Dictionary.

[56] A *Sipahi* was a man who, by virtue of war and being conquered, had a contractual agreement with the Sultan to obey him in matters of boundaries and war.

[57] https://www.answering-islam.org/authors/cornelius/makr.html

[58] Euzebije Fermendzin, ed. *Acta Bosnae Potissimum ecclesiastica cum inserito editors documentorum registi ab sono 925 usque ad annum 1752* (Zagreb: Academia Scientiarum et Artium Slavorum Meridionalium, 1982), p. 144

[59] Although these advisors to the Sultan hatched plans, and Saruca was exiled, eventually Fazlullah was discovered to have made himself wealthy and Saruca was found to be loyal. Saruca was brought back, and Fazlullah disposed of. *The Holy Wars of King Wladislas and Sultan Murad*' by John Jefferson (2012) p.327

[60] The Jewish Encyclopedia: a descriptive record of the history, religion, literature, and customs of the Jewish people from the earliest times to the present day, Vol.2 Isidore Singer, Cyrus Adler, Funk and Wagnalls, 1912 p.460

[61] World History - Volume 1 by David Coomb- Page 119

[62] Some Muslims still adhere to Shari'a according to its legal terms and continue to take slaves, as we see demonstrated amongst Wahhabist, ISIS, Boko Haram, and other groups whom non-Muslims tend to term as terrorists, but who are, in fact, only being loyal to their Scriptures.

[63] Bernard Lewis, Race and Color in Islam (New York and London: Harper Torchbooks, 1971),op. cit., p. 97

[64] Murray Gordon, Slavery in the Arab World, New Amsterdam Press, New York, 1989. Originally published in French by Editions R.obert Laffont, S.A. Paris, 1987, page 28.

[65] "Fischer W. Alan (1978) The sale of slaves in the Ottoman Empire: Markets and state taxes on slave sales, some preliminary considerations. Bogazici Universitesi Dergisi, Beseri Bilimler - Humanities, vol. 6, pp. 150-151

[66] Mackie, Gerry (December 1996). "Ending Footbinding and Infibulation: A Convention Account" (PDF). American Sociological Review. 61 (6): 999–1017. doi:10.2307/2096305

[67] David D. Laitin (1 May 1977). Politics, Language, and Thought: The Somali Experience. University of Chicago Press. pp. 29–30. ISBN 978-0-226-46791-7.

[68] Susi O'Neill. "The blood of a nation of Slaves in Stone Town". www.pilotguides.com. Globe Trekker. Archived from the original on December 25, 2008.

[69] "Travels in Nubia, by John Lewis Burc.khardt". Ebooks.adelaide.edu.au 2015-08-25.

[70] Kwame Anthony Appiah; Henry Louis Gates (2005). Africana: The Encyclopedia of the African and African-American Experience 5-Volume Set. Oxford University Press. p. 295. ISBN 0195170555. and David Livingstone (2006). "The Last Journals of David Livingstone, in Central Africa, from 1865 to His Death". Echo Library. p.46. ISBN 1-84637-555-X

[71] Stanley Henry M., How I Found Livingstone; travels, adventures, and discoveries in Central Africa, including an account of four months' residence with Dr. Livingstone. (1871)

[72] Campbell, Gwyn (2004). Abolition and Its Aftermath in the Indian Ocean Africa and Asia. Psychology Press. p. 121. ISBN 0203493028.

[73] Murray Gordon, Slavery in the Arab World, New Amsterdam Press, New York, 1989. Originally published in French by Editions Robert Laffont, S.A. Paris, 1987 p.111 and A. Adu Boahen, "The Caravan Trade in the Nineteenth Century,"Journal ofAfrican History, vol. 3, no. 2 (1962), p. 351.

[74] ibid p.92

[75] The Holy Wars of King Wladislas and Sultan Murad: The Ottoman-Christian Conflict from 1438-1444 (History of Warfare) p.83

[76] https://www.pilotguides.com/articles/the-blood-of-a-nation-of-slaves-in-stone-town/

[77] Ochieng', William Robert (1975). Eastern Kenya and Its Invaders. East African Literature Bureau. p. 76. Retrieved 15 May 2015., Bethwell A. Ogot, Zamani: A Survey of East African History, (East African Publishing House: 1974), p.104, Lodhi, Abdulaziz (2000). Oriental influences in Swahili: a study in language and culture contacts. Acta Universitatis Gothoburgensis. p. 17. ISBN 9173463779.

[78] Gwyn Campbell, The Structure of Slavery in Indian Ocean Africa and Asia, 1 edition, (Routledge: 2003), p.ix

[79] Rodriguez, Junius P. (2007). Encyclopedia of Slave Resistance and Rebellion, Volume 2. Greenwood Publishing Group. p. 585. ISBN 0313332738.

[80] "Islam, From Arab To Islamic Empire: The Early Abbasid Era". History-world.org. Retrieved 2016-03-23.

[81] Kevin Shillington, ed. (2005), Encyclopedia of African History, CRC Press, vol. 1, pp. 333–34; Nicolas Argenti (2007), The Intestines of the State: Youth, Violence and Belated Histories in the Cameroon Grassfields, University of Chicago Press, p. 42.

[82]Davis, Robert C. (2003). Christian Slaves, Muslim Masters: White Slavery in the Mediterranean, the Barbary Coast and Italy, 1500-1800. Palgrave Macmillan. ISBN 978-0-333-71966-4.

[83] Adams, Charles Hansford (2005). The Narrative of Robert Adams: A Barbary Captive. New York: Cambridge University Press. pp. xlv–xlvi. ISBN 978-0-521-603-73-7.

[84] Diego de Haedo, Topografía e historia general de Argel, 3 vols., Madrid, 1927-29.

243 The Cambridge World History of Slavery: Volume 3, AD 1420–AD 1804

[86] James William Brodman. ""Ransoming Captives in Crusader Spain: The Order of Merced on the Christian-Islamic Frontier"". Libro.uca.edu. Retrieved 2016-03-23., Mikhail Kizilov. "Slave Trade in the Early Modern Crimea From the Perspective of Christian, Muslim, and Jewish Sources". Oxford University. pp. 7–28.

[87] Brodman, James William, Ransoming Captives in Crusader Spain:The Order of Merced on the Christian-Islamic Frontier, 1986

[88] Hitchens, Christopher (2007-01-09). "Jefferson's Quran". Slate. ISSN 1091-2339.

[89] The Thomas Jefferson Papers - America and the Barbary Pirates - (American Memory from the Library of Congress)

[90] The Cambridge World History of Slavery: Volume 3, AD 1420–AD 1804

[91] Noble, David Cook. "Nicolás de Ovando" in Encyclopedia of Latin American History and Culture, vol.4, p. 254. New York: Charles Scribner's Sons 1996.

[92] Patrick Manning, "The Slave Trade: The Formal Dermographics of a Global System" in Joseph E. Inikori and Stanley L. Engerman (eds), The Atlantic Slave Trade: Effects on Economies, Societies and Peoples in Africa, the Americas, and Europe (Duke University Press, 1992), pp. 117-44

[93] https://www.answering-islam.org/Green/slavery.htm
https://www.answering-islam.org/authors/thomas/slavery.html
https://www.samaa.tv/global/2017/10/isis-among-terrorist-groups-using-slaves-recruit-rapists-domestic-abusers/
https://www.hrw.org/news/2015/09/05/slavery-isis-rules#

Ꝺara Ḫâtûn

[94] πίλεον λευκόν, Diodorus Siculus Exc. Leg. 22 p. 625, ed. Wess.; Plaut. Amphit. I.1.306; Persius, V.82

[95] ibid, Optatus, De sch. Don., Appendix 8

[96] Mikhail Kizilov. "Slave Trade in the Early Modern Crimea From the Perspective of Christian, Muslim, and Jewish Sources". Oxford University. pp. 7–28.

[97] Blue Guide, Turkey" A&C Black, 2001, p. 77

[98] Dariusz Kołodziejczyk, as reported by Mikhail Kizilov (2007). "Slaves, Money Lenders, and Prisoner Guards:The Jews and the Trade in Slaves and Captivesin the Crimean Khanate". The Journal of Jewish Studies. p. 2.

[99] https://www.answering-islam.org/Silas/slavery.htm

[100] Bukhari (Book #52, Hadith #220)

[101] "Horrible Traffic in Circassian Women - Infanticide in Turkey" New York Daily Times, August 6, 1856 and Http://en.wikipedia.org/wiki/Circassian_beauties

[102] "Horrible Traffic in Circassian Women - Infanticide in Turkey" New York Daily Times, August 6, 1856

[103] About Turkey Burak Sansal http://www.allaboutturkey.com/harem.htm

[104] http://raymondibrahim.com/2011/05/31/raped-and-ransacked-in-the-muslim-world/

[105] http://www.alarabiya.net/articles/2011/06/04/151770.html

[106] "It is permissible to have sexual intercourse with the female captive. Allah the almighty said: '[Successful are the believers] who guard their chastity, except from their wives or the captives and slaves that their right hands possess, for then they are free from blame [Koran 23:5-6] 4:24 And forbidden to you are wedded wives of other people except those who have fallen in your hands (as prisoners of war) . . . (Sayyid A'La Abul Maududi, The Meaning of the Quran, vol. 1, p. 319).
O Prophet! Lo! We have made lawful unto thee thy wives unto whom thou hast paid their dowries, and those whom thy right hand possesseth of those whom Allah hath given thee as spoils of war, and the daughters of thine uncle on the father's side and the daughters of thine aunts on the father's side, and the daughters of thine uncle on the mother's side and the daughters of thine aunts on the mother's side who emigrated with thee, those whom their right hands possess - that thou mayst be free from blame, for Allah is ever Forgiving, Merciful." Quran Sura (verse). 33:50 translated by Pickthall

www.ingramcontent.com/pod-product-compliance
Lightning Source LLC
Chambersburg PA
CBHW060212030726
47499CB00004B/1019